NIGHT AND DAY

ANNE
STUART

GAYLE WILSON

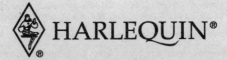

HARLEQUIN®

TORONTO • NEW YORK • LONDON
AMSTERDAM • PARIS • SYDNEY • HAMBURG
STOCKHOLM • ATHENS • TOKYO • MILAN • MADRID
PRAGUE • WARSAW • BUDAPEST • AUCKLAND

ISBN 0-373-22637-3

NIGHT AND DAY

Copyright © 2001 by Harlequin Books S.A.

The publisher acknowledges the copyright holders
of the individual works as follows:

NIGHT
Copyright © 2001 by Anne Kristine Stuart Ohlrogge

DAY
Copyright © 2001 by Mona Gay Thomas

Visit us at www.eHarlequin.com

Printed in U.S.A.

Dear Reader,

This holiday season, deck the halls with some of the most exciting names in romantic suspense: Anne Stuart *and* Gayle Wilson. These two award-winning authors have returned together to Harlequin Intrigue to reprise their much loved miniseries—CATSPAW and MEN OF MYSTERY—in a special 2-in-1 collection. *Night and Day* is a guaranteed keeper and the best stocking stuffer around!

Find out what happens when a single-dad secret agent has to protect a beautiful scientist as our MONTANA CONFIDENTIAL series continues with *Licensed To Marry* by Charlotte Douglas.

The *stork* is coming down the chimney this year, as Joanna Wayne begins a brand-new series of books set in the sultry South. Look for *Another Woman's Baby* this month and more HIDDEN PASSIONS books to come in the near future.

Also available from Harlequin Intrigue is the second title in Susan Kearney's HIDE AND SEEK trilogy. The search goes on in *Hidden Hearts*.

Happy holidays from all of us at Harlequin Intrigue.

Sincerely,

Denise O'Sullivan
Associate Senior Editor
Harlequin Intrigue

P.S.—Next month you can find *another* special holiday title—*A Woman with a Mystery* by B.J. Daniels

Dear Reader,

It's been a special treat for me to visit the world of Patrick Blackheart and company again. He first made an appearance in a Harlequin Intrigue novel in 1985 (*Catspaw*, Intrigue #9), returned in *Catspaw* II in 1988 (Harlequin Intrigue #103) and he's been waiting for a chance to come back. This time he's got a full-grown son, and Michael's story forms the first half of our duet.

When Michael Blackheart discovers who his real father is, he decides revenge and a spot of larceny are just the thing. Throw in some stolen Nazi treasures, neo-Nazi bad guys and a long-legged blonde who's just about the most luscious thing he's ever seen, and he gets more than he bargained for.

It's been fun to be writing for Harlequin Intrigue again, and a real pleasure to work with Gayle Wilson, who has to be one of my favorite writers. But I'll let her tell you about her story....

I was so delighted to be asked to create another Man of Mystery for Harlequin Intrigue. The first book in this series about an elite and secretive CIA antiterrorist team won the Romance Writers of America's RITA Award last year for Best Romantic Suspense in 2000.

And of course I absolutely jumped at the chance of working with the glorious Anne Stuart.

In this novella, Duncan Culhane carries on the MEN OF MYSTERY tradition of high adventure and strong romance, but in the course of that, you get to look forward to him encountering the legendary Patrick Blackheart. Maybe Harlequin Intrigue should have called this one *The Cat Burglar and the Spy*. They settled instead for the equally revealing and most appropriate *Night and Day*.

Anne Stuart   Gayle Wilson

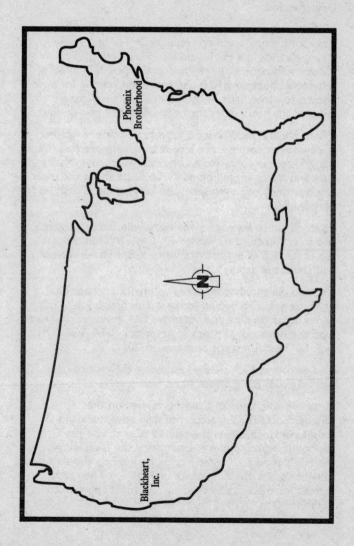

CAST OF CHARACTERS

Michael Blackheart—Long-lost son of a world famous jewel thief, he's unwittingly followed in his father's footsteps. Now he's out for revenge.

Isabel Linden—Jack Helms's executive assistant, she's in the wrong place at the wrong time.

Patrick Blackheart—World famous jewel thief turned security expert, out to protect the famous Norenheld Treasure from thieves, unaware that the main threat comes from the son he never knew.

Ferris (Francesca) Blackheart—Patrick's wife.

Jack Helms—A computer billionaire who's auctioning off the Norenheld Treasure, he has too many secrets.

Henry Johnson—Helms's top gofer, a man who will stop at nothing to do his master's bidding.

* * *

Griff Cabot—When the head of the Phoenix Brotherhood sends one of his top agents to do a favor for an old friend, his only intent is some long-delayed matchmaking. He has no idea of the dangerous implications his request will have for both of them.

Andrea Sorrenson—An attempt to retrieve her grandmother's music box thrusts Andrea into the world of international terrorism that claimed her husband's life five years ago.

Duncan Culhane—His last mission for the CIA's elite External Security Team resulted in the death of his partner. When Duncan meets Paul Sorrenson's widow, he is as haunted by the memory of what was once between them as by his guilt over her husband's death.

For Gay, a wonderful writer
and a gracious, long-suffering collaborator.

NIGHT
ANNE STUART

ABOUT THE AUTHOR

Anne Stuart has written over sixty novels in her twenty-five-plus years as a romance novelist. She's won every major award in the business, including three RITA Awards from Romance Writers of America, as well as their Lifetime Achievement Award. Anne's books have made various bestseller lists, and she has been quoted in *People, USA Today* and *Vogue*. She has also appeared on *Entertainment Tonight,* and, according to her, done her best to cause trouble! When she's not writing or traveling around the country speaking to various writers' groups, she can be found at home in northern Vermont, with her husband, two children, a dog and three cats.

Books by Anne Stuart

HARLEQUIN INTRIGUE
009—CATSPAW
059—HAND IN GLOVE
103—CATSPAW II
329—WINTER'S EDGE
637—NIGHT AND DAY
       "Night"

Don't miss any of our special offers. Write to us at the following address for information on our newest releases.

Harlequin Reader Service
U.S.: 3010 Walden Ave., P.O. Box 1325, Buffalo, NY 14269
Canadian: P.O. Box 609, Fort Erie, Ont. L2A 5X3

Chapter One

When Michael Blackheart opened his eyes the bedroom was bathed in twilight shadows. He didn't move, orienting himself to his surroundings with the ease of a cat. He'd arrived from London a mere seven hours ago, and once he'd checked into his suite at the Carlyle Hotel he'd gone straight to bed, falling into the kind of instant, dreamless sleep that had always been there at his command.

He'd woken up on time as well, not needing an alarm clock or a wake-up call. It was six o'clock in the evening, San Francisco time, and he had a fortune to steal. It was going to be a busy night.

He showered and dressed with his automatic deliberation, then sat down for a leisurely meal provided by the Carlyle's excellent room service. He probably wouldn't get a chance to eat for the next eighteen hours, and he never underestimated his body's need for fuel. This time tomorrow he'd be on his way back to Europe, a great deal richer. In the meantime, he had a job to do.

His suite had a balcony, and he stepped out into the brisk autumn air. He'd always liked San Francisco—the cool, temperate climate, the steep hills and the smell of the bay. He felt an odd sort of affinity for the place. Never knowing that it should have been home.

He looked down into the busy streets. In another hour limousines would be pulling up to the front portico of the Carlyle, dispensing their elegantly clothed passengers. For now it was just the working stiffs bustling around down there, with the added annoyance of several television trucks. It was a minor inconvenience. He'd managed before, in the full glare of television lights. This would only add piquancy to his challenge.

He stepped back from the railing, staring up at the sky. It was foggy, almost misting, and he smiled faintly. He liked the darkness and the rain, the night and all the shadows. He was a creature of the night, always had been, always would be. This was where he belonged.

In the meantime, however, he had to concentrate on why he was here. The Norenheld Treasure was about to be auctioned off tomorrow evening, and tonight a preview and reception was being held in the hotel ballroom beneath him. By the time they finally got around to taking bids, there would be very little left to bid on.

It was his last big score, and he intended to go out with a bang. A huge, daring theft that left the police, the venerable auction house, Southworth, and the private security firm both frustrated and baffled. The private security firm of Blackheart, Inc., his esteemed father.

If it hadn't been for Uncle Felix he wouldn't have even known he still had a father. And masterworks of jewelry and painting would have held no allure for a man with his history—been there, done that. He thought he had nothing left to prove, to himself or anyone else. He'd been a con man, a thief, an artist of duplicity for most of his twenty-nine years, and he'd been ready to leave it all behind, find some sort of peaceful occupation.

Until he discovered he had a father after all.

It had been an act of rash sentimentality, tracking down his great uncle. Felix was from his grandmother's side of the family, one of the great Gypsy families of northern Europe, and Felix, as one of the last remaining members, wisely kept a low profile. He was very old—near ninety, and he'd managed to evade the police for his entire life. Michael hadn't been quite so lucky—the last robbery had been botched, not by his own incompetence but by the greed and weakness of his partner, and when push came to shove, Marybeth had turned him in, rather than take the fall herself.

He'd been phlegmatic about it. He'd learned the art of the con from his grandfather, perfected it over the years with the help of aunts and uncles, including the venerable Uncle Felix, and the short prison term he'd drawn was long overdue.

And he thought he'd strolled out of the French corrections center a changed man, ready to turn his energies to new endeavors. He no longer craved the adrenaline rush, and somehow the notion of gentleman thief had worn thin.

Until he'd met with Uncle Felix in a café in Budapest and heard the words that would change his life once more.

"Retire?" Felix had echoed, his thick accent almost impenetrable. "Why should a young man like you do such a thing? You've trained in a profession, you're one of the best living. Why turn your back on all that talent?"

"It's not a profession, Uncle, it's a criminal career," Michael had replied.

"You're afraid of getting caught? Lost your nerve? I wouldn't have thought it of you, my boy. You always had nerves of steel. Prison's just part of the game we play—you can't take a short stretch like that so seriously."

"Easy for you to say," Michael said. "You were never caught."

"Not by the police," Felix agreed. "The police are nothing. I survived the Nazis—a far trickier feat, since they wanted to wipe out my kind."

"I never knew you were Jewish," Michael said, teasing.

"The gypsies, boy. The Nazis had three targets— Jews, gypsies and homosexuals. It's amazing there's any creativity left in Europe after their holocaust."

"It was a long time ago, Uncle."

"We never forget. No one should ever forget," he said.

The old man's hand was shaking as he lit one of his strong, foul-smelling cigarettes, and he glanced at Michael across his tiny cup of coffee. "So what will you do, then? Become an accountant? A bureaucrat?"

Michael had shrugged. "There's no hurry. I have a bit of money put aside that no one was able to find—I'll be all right for the time being. I just wanted to tell you my decision, since you're the head of the family."

"Damned small family by now," Felix had muttered. "I hate to see our tradition swallowed up by convention. If only your mother had lived…"

"But she didn't, Uncle. She died with my father in that car accident, before I was even three. If it wasn't for you and Grandfather I would have been put in an institution. I've discovered I don't like institutions," he added with a faint smile.

Felix shook his head. "I might as well tell you, then," he said obscurely.

"Tell me what?"

"I had one last job for you. I was going to send for you when I got your phone call. The perfect job, one that settles old scores and leaves you wealthy."

"I have no old scores to settle, and I've got enough money for the time being."

"No one ever has enough money," Felix said. "If it's more than you need, give it where it's needed. The people you take it from don't deserve to have it."

"So you and Grandfather always told me," Michael said. "Maybe you're right, but I've decided it's no longer up to me to make those judgments."

Felix stared at him, his ancient face creased in frustration. After a moment he nodded, as if coming to some internal decision. "Then I won't tell you about the job," he said. "You're better off not knowing and not being tempted."

"Much better," Michael said. His uncle was baiting a trap for him; Michael knew the signs well. Felix was a master at getting what he wanted, and he was going to pull out all the stops. It would be fascinating to watch, as long as he kept clear of temptation.

"And why should you care about what the Germans did to your family? The number of people they killed. There would be more than just you and me left if it weren't for those butchers."

"Uncle…" He was doing a good job of it, but Michael had no intention of being suckered in by him.

"Don't worry," Felix said mournfully. "As you said, it was all long ago. Thirty years since you were born and your father took off. Time to forgive and forget."

The trap was set and baited, and all his great-uncle had to do was wait for Michael to reach for it. If he had any sense at all he would toss some money on the table to pay for the coffee, kiss Felix's leathery cheek and wish him good luck.

But curiosity had always been his besetting sin. "My father?" he echoed. "He didn't take off—he was a race car driver. He died in an accident." And he thought he heard the clang of the trap snapping shut around him.

"That's what they told you. Paulus had always insisted you be spared the truth. He didn't want the man showing up, trying to claim you once your mother had passed on. He wasn't a race car driver, my boy, and he isn't dead. He's a thief, just like you and me, alive and well and living in San Francisco.''

Michael was so schooled at hiding his reactions that he didn't even blink. It didn't matter—he couldn't fool Felix. ''So he's alive,'' he said after a moment. ''Why should I care one way or the other?'' Maybe it was a noose tightening around his neck, rather than a trap. But Uncle Felix wouldn't want him dead. He just wanted his own way.

''Because he abandoned you and your mother, and she never loved another man afterward. Don't you think a man should take responsibility for the children he fathers?''

''I really don't give a damn.''

''He's turned his back on his profession as well. Perhaps you're more like him than I thought.''

''What do you mean by that?''

''He's not a thief anymore. He's a security consultant—he catches thieves and puts them away. Thieves like you, Michael. His company has been hired to do the security for an auction being held in San Francisco. The Norenheld Treasure. Ever heard of it?''

''Who hasn't? It's the collection of that computer millionaire's Norwegian uncle. Old masters, jewelry, books and artwork worth a fortune. So the rich man wants to get richer. I told you, I don't care.''

''What if I told you that the Norenheld Treasure is an elaborate charade, and the artwork comes from William Helms's grandfather, not his uncle? That the provenances on everything have been carefully doc-tored—when you have the kind of money Helms has, anything is possible.''

"And why would he want to do that?''

"So he can sell the stuff and make a fortune with-out the original owners making a fuss.''

"They're stolen? We're thieves, Uncle. Why should we care if stolen artwork gets resold?''

"Because Helms's grandfather was Wilhelm von Helmich. You've heard of him, haven't you?''

"The Butcher of Berlin? Yes.''

"One of the S.S. generals who escaped, with a for-tune in stolen artwork.''

"And you know this for a fact?''

Felix had shrugged. "Who can be sure of any-thing?''

"Very sad, Uncle, but as you said, the original owners are all dead. It's too late to do them any good.''

"Which means you can take the stuff with a clear conscience. Since you suddenly decided to develop one at this stage in the game.''

Michael shook his head. "It doesn't matter to me that some war criminal's offspring gets the money. He wasn't the one who committed the crimes.''

"And what if I told you I'd heard rumors that the money is going to support neo-Nazi activities?''

Clang. The trap sprang shut, like a vise around his throat. He made one last feeble attempt to fight. "I never get involved in politics.''

But Felix knew he had him. "It's child's play to a man of your talents. You remove the Norenheld Treasure before it can be auctioned off, you deprive Nazi spawn of their ill-gotten gains, you keep the money from falling into the hands of terrorists, and you settle a score against the man who fathered and abandoned you. And you end up a very rich man. How can you refuse?''

Uncle Felix stubbed out his cigarette, then reached for the crumpled pack. For the first time in Michael's life he wished he smoked.

''It won't be easy, of course,'' Uncle Felix continued. ''But when is anything worthwhile easy? You can do it—we raised you right, your grandfather and me, gave you the knowledge and skills of generations of thieves. I've already done the preliminary research—I've got schematics of the alarm system and some interesting little technological toys that interfere with security tapes. I also have the layout of the hotel where the reception will be held. That seems like the best time to take the treasure.''

''In the full sight of the public?''

''You always liked a challenge,'' Felix said with a grin. ''The reception is on the 29th of October. The next day everything is moved back to Southworth's auction house for the actual sale, and their security is hardwired into the system. Besides, then it's no longer Blackheart's responsibility, and that's half the lure, isn't it?''

''You sound like you think I'm going to do it.''

''I brought you up, Michael. I know you well. You'll do it. And there's no cut for me this time. My reward will be the pleasure in knowing it's done.''

"Noble of you," Michael murmured. "And if I'm caught?"

"There's not a prison that can hold you. We both know that. I always wondered why you decided to serve out your sentence in France, when there was no need."

"I decided it was my time," Michael said. "Every now and then you have to pay the piper."

"Well, right now you're paid ahead. It's a noble thing you're doing, Michael."

"I didn't say I'd do it."

"But you will," said Uncle Felix.

Michael's smile was slow and rueful. "But I will," he agreed.

A MONTH LATER HE WAS STILL regretting his decision. One last haul had seemed an excellent idea in the beginning, with the added benefit of paying off a few scores along the way. He could already feel the adrenaline pumping in his veins, and he knew regret was the last thing he needed tonight. He was about to take center stage in a drama, and he planned to come out on the other side the winner.

He didn't bother to check his reflection in the mirror as he left his suite. He already knew what he looked like. He wore evening clothes better than most men his age—he had a long, lean body that looked good in Armani. He could either blend in or stand out, depending on his mood. Tonight it would be a little of both.

The first task was getting into the reception in the first place. It was by invitation only, and all the guests had had their net worth vetted long before they were allowed into the ballroom. Southworth didn't want to waste their time or their expensive canapés on people who couldn't afford to bid.

He had no idea whether the old man was going to be there or not, and that added a nice edge to his pleasurable tension. Would he meet his long-lost father for the first time, just as he was robbing him blind? One could only hope.

He strolled down to the elegant lobby of the old hotel. Another point in his favor—they'd chosen one of San Francisco's venerable old hotels, rather than one of the new high rises with wired-in security. The Carlyle had been updated and remodeled, but its very age and quirkiness made it a much more likely candidate for robbery than one of those angular, window-strewn boxes.

It also helped that Southworth was holding the reception outside the environs of their auction house. They were counting on a huge media presence, and while their largest rooms could accommodate the number of potential bidders here tonight, they couldn't hold those same people milling around drinking champagne.

No, Uncle Felix was right, this job was tailor-made for him. The time for regret was past. The time for action was now.

But first he had to get through the security at the wide double doors to the ballroom.

ISABEL LINDEN WAS SEETHING beneath her calm exterior. This day, in fact, the last month had been noth-

ing but a long line of disasters, and she'd finally
reached the breaking point. Ten months as William
Helms's assistant had taken its toll on her. She should
have known that the job and salary were too good to
be true.

She liked her work, and always had. She had the
true gift of being able to bring chaos out of order,
and for five years she'd run her own consulting firm,
helping harassed executives find structure in their
lives. She shouldn't have listened to temptation, to
the siren call of Bill Helms himself, one of the
world's richest men. He'd wanted her to take on the
job of organizing his business and social life, and the
money and prestige had been too good to refuse.

She should have refused it. For one thing, Helms
barely let her near anything interesting in his office.
There was almost an air of secrecy about half of what
he did, which was ridiculous, considering the kind of
press coverage he usually got.

For another, she had discovered that she really
didn't like nerdy little billionaires who thought their
vast amounts of money made them witty and attractive and incapable of mistakes. Particularly one who
looked at her five-foot-ten-inch, blond-haired, buxom
frame and practically drooled. He was always finding
excuses to lean over her, touch her, and yet for some
reason he never actually came out and asked her for
a date. Probably because he knew she'd say no.

Probably because he knew it would give her the
excuse to quit, something she'd been longing to do
since she first took the job in January.

But damn, it was hard to walk away from that much money.

She was going to do it, though. She wanted nothing more than to quit that very night, but she was a calm, organized person and knew perfectly well that she needed to wait for the light of day and put it in writing. None of this "take this job and shove it" stuff, no matter how tempting. Not with someone as powerful as Bill Helms.

She had a killer headache, caused by the high-pitched noise of the crowd of well-dressed people surrounding her, by the clink of glasses and the hassle of trying to wiggle into her slinky silver dress in the tiny bathroom stall of the old hotel, caused by the weight of her thick blond hair, pinned into a heavy chignon at the base of her neck. Her feet in the four-inch heels hurt as well. She wanted to kick off her shoes, shake her hair free and run out of the crowded, noisy room.

She did no such thing, of course. Her job was to serve as hostess, to keep an eye on things, make sure everything went smoothly, and she'd do just that. Tomorrow she'd quit.

So she smiled, and chatted, and mingled, doing her best to be utterly charming, until she turned around and came face-to-face with a stranger, and was momentarily speechless. The only word that came to her startled brain was nemesis.

Chapter Two

Isabel knew every one of the four hundred people in the crowded ballroom, either by name or reputation. She'd personally gone over the list of guests three times to double-check the auction house's proposal, and that man definitely wasn't on it.

She held her glass of champagne in one hand, listening to the ancient industrialist babble on about his newest art acquisition, and all the time she watched the newcomer like a hawk.

He was gorgeous, no question about that. Taller than she was, which was a blessing, and then she could have kicked herself. A blessing? Why the hell should it matter if a gate-crasher was tall?

"That's fascinating," she murmured to the industrialist, sipping her champagne, watching the stranger. He was moving through the ballroom at a leisurely pace, with no seeming destination in mind, and a moment later he disappeared into the crowd.

He was probably there with one of the vetted

guests, Isabel told herself. With his wife or lover, prepared to spend a fortune on Bill Helms's inherited art treasures. Blackheart, Inc.'s security firm was impeccable—there was no way they would have allowed an uninvited guest past the doors of the ballroom, not with millions of dollars worth of artwork just lying out.

Not that they weren't protected, she reminded herself. If anyone moved or touched anything an ear-splitting alarm would go off, striking terror into the hearts of all around. She knew because she'd reached out to adjust the charming Lalique music box, curious to hear what song it played.

So really, she could dismiss the fascinating stranger, concentrate on charming the industrialist and his sour-looking wife, sip her champagne and enjoy herself. Her job was done, and would soon be over. She could relax.

"Excuse me," she said, interrupting the old man. "There's someone I must see."

She kept her champagne glass in her hand as she threaded her way through the crowds. There were a number of tall men in the room. Even Patrick Blackheart, retired jewel thief and security consultant extraordinaire, was taller than she was.

But she found herself heading for the music box, drawn to it as she was before, and her instincts served her well. He was standing there, staring at it, a bemused expression on his face.

"Charming, isn't it?" she said.

He turned to look down at her, and she got the full force of his brown eyes. Gorgeous didn't begin to describe him. He had a narrow, clever face, full of planes and angles, a strong nose, a wry, cynical mouth. His dark blond hair was too long, but on him it looked good. Hell, on him anything would have looked good, Isabel thought with an inward sigh. Why couldn't millionaires look like him, with devilish eyes and a tall, elegant body?

Of course, he probably was a millionaire to be able to get into this reception, she reminded herself. But what were the chances that someone would be rich, gorgeous, unattached and straight? Not likely.

"Charming," he said. Oh, God, he had an accent as well! Just a faint one, but hardly fair when she was already feeling vulnerable. "I didn't know Lalique made music boxes."

"I gather this might be the only one." Isabel took a sip of her champagne. It was room temperature, the bubbles gone, but she still felt slightly giddy looking up at him.

"What tune does it play?"

"I don't know. Actually I tried to see and set off all the alarms," she added wryly. "By the way, I'm Isabel Linden, Bill Helms's executive assistant. And you are…?"

"Michael," he said. "Michael Blackheart."

He'd managed to startle her. "Blackheart? Are you part of the security…?"

"Just a coincidence," he said lightly. "We're not related. So tell me, Isabel, what's your favorite piece in this collection? I like that small Rembrandt, and the Vermeer is tempting, though I'm not sure how well it would go on my wall."

Definitely a millionaire, if he thought he could afford to have the Vermeer on his wall. Or a liar. "I like the music box," she said. "It's not worth as much as a lot of the other stuff—the Rembrandt's probably the most valuable, followed by the two Renoirs and the Vermeer. I do love the Vermeer as well," she added with a covetous sigh. "But the music box touches me."

"As long as you don't touch it," he said with a faint smile. "Shall we see what happens if we do?"

"I told you, all hell breaks loose," Isabel said.

"I don't know if I've ever seen all hell breaking loose. Besides, I want to know what song it plays. Whether it's still working. I wouldn't want to bid on something that was broken."

"You're intending to bid on the music box?" she asked, fascinated. He didn't seem the type to be interested in such a whimsical, delicate piece. "Did you read the card—the piece has been withdrawn? I don't know if there was a private, pre-emptive bid or if Mr. Helms changed his mind, but it's not for sale."

"Everything's for sale, if you're willing to pay the price," he said calmly. And before she could stop him he reached out and picked up the delicate crystal box.

All hell was an understatement. The lighting in the ballroom had been subtle, muted, with spotlights trained on the various objets d'art. Now bright lights flashed on overhead, a piercing alarm silenced the small dance band in the corner, and everyone froze as an army of men crossed the room in lead-footed haste, surrounding Isabel and her dangerous new acquaintance. Not Blackheart's staff, she realized, but Helms's hand-picked security.

"Calm down, boys," Michael said in an easy voice, totally undisturbed by the fuss he'd created. "You wouldn't want to make me drop it, now would you?"

The screech of the alarms stopped abruptly, and the silence in the room was shocking. The only sound was the faint, delicate melody emanating from the crystal box in Michael Blackheart's large, graceful hands.

Michael closed the tiny crystal lid and set the box down on the velvet dais that had been artfully created by the Southworth minions. "If I were trying to steal it I'd hardly do it in a roomful of people," he said wryly. "Sorry to make such a fuss."

"It's all right, Johnson," Isabel said to the beefy head of Bill Helms's security. "He's with me."

Henry Johnson didn't look convinced, but there was nothing he could do without making a scene. The band had started playing again, people were talking once more, and the lights had returned to their normal muted hues. "Mr. Helms won't like it," he said darkly.

"I'll explain it to him. It was just an unfortunate accident," she said smoothly. She was good at that, smoothing ruffled feathers, and even Johnson managed to be lulled. He didn't like her, she knew that. She suspected he didn't like much of anyone, but he still managed to react the way she wanted him to.

Without a word he turned on his heels and left,

followed by the five tall blond men who always seemed to shadow him. She should know their names by now, but they all had those sort of anonymous American names like Smith and Jones and Brown and Johnson. She tended to think of them as window dressing, part of Bill Helms's interior decorating, though she always thought they were an odd choice. All those tall, stalwart blond men made Bill Helms's nerdy exterior look even more unprepossessing.

She turned back to Michael Blackheart, who was looking completely unchastened. "Am I?" he said in a curious voice.

"Are you what?"

"With you?"

She managed not to flush, though she wanted to. "Better with me than with Helms's goons. That wasn't a very smart thing to do."

"I'm not very good at following rules. What are you to Bill Helms?"

"Nothing!" she said, too quickly. "That is, I work for him. I told you, I'm his executive assistant. At least, for now."

"You think he's going to fire you?"

"I'm going to quit. It's not really my thing."

"And what is your thing?"

He wasn't standing that close to her, and yet she found herself acutely aware of him. It must be the exhaustion, the champagne, the stress playing games with her mind. She stared up at him in silence for a moment, daydreaming.

"My thing?" she echoed dazedly.

"What is it you do?"

"I'm good at organizing people. At creating order out of chaos."

"Sounds like a useful talent. Except for those who prefer chaos."

"And you're one of those people?" she asked.

He shrugged. "I like adrenaline. I'm trying to wean myself away from it, though. A little order might come in handy, and you're going to need a job. When do you finish with Helms?"

"Tonight," she said, not even knowing she was going to say that. She tried to pull herself together. No more champagne, my girl. No more looking into those devastating brown eyes. "What kind of business do you have, Mr. Blackheart?"

"Call me Michael. You wouldn't want to get me confused with a retired jewel thief, now would you?" he said lightly.

Isabel laughed. "You've obviously heard of Blackheart, Inc. I know it seems bizarre, but he's the best in the business."

"I can imagine. He learned it from the inside," Michael said.

"So you haven't told me what kind of business you have. What is it you'd like me to do for you?"

For a moment he didn't say a word. He just looked at her, and she felt herself slip into his gaze like sliding into a warm pool of water.

And then he smiled, that faint, elegant smile that promised nothing and everything. "Give me a few hours to think about it."

9:00 p.m.

SHE WAS DEFINITELY a complication, Michael thought, sipping the ginger ale in the champagne glass. He'd learned early on that he worked best hungry and sober, and not even Southworth's lavish spread could tempt him. The only temptation in the place, besides millions and millions of dollars worth of stolen art treasures, was Miss Isabel Linden. She could distract a saint in search of something, a sinner in search of redemption. He was neither—redemption was an overrated commodity, and sainthood was probably dead boring. He had no intention of discovering whether it was or not.

And unfortunately, he had no intention of doing more with Miss Isabel Linden than allow himself a stray erotic fantasy. He had a job to do, and he never mixed business with pleasure.

She liked that music box, a fact which charmed him. Most of the women he knew would have been drawn to the most valuable stuff, the old masters, or the gold and jewelry. He could imagine her in that ornate, seventeenth-century pearl parure from Venice, the creamy tones of the pearls glistening against her luscious skin, but the fact was, he'd never know. It would have to be one of those lost opportunities that were far more delightful in the abstract than in reality. If this were a different night, if he managed to get her in bed, she'd probably be...

Absolutely irresistible, he admitted, watching her covertly from across the room. She'd been circulating, charming the rich old men, flattering the rich old ladies, keeping everything running smoothly, and he could see she was very good at her job. Bringing order out of chaos. Not that appealing for a man who had always thrived on chaos, of course, but there was still something about her that drew him, and it wasn't just her tall, luscious body. It was the sense of calm. It made him want to bury himself in her, lose himself in her silky, soothing body, feel her arms around him, rest his head on her breasts, slide between her legs...

Damn. He turned on his heel, too abruptly, bumping into a small, pretty woman. He caught his champagne glass in time, and hers as well, avoiding disaster.

"Terribly sorry," he said, about to move away.

"You're very agile," the woman said in a husky voice. "I thought you might be."

That caught his attention. He looked down at her—she was plump, elegantly put together, and probably ten years older than he was. He was used to being hit on by bored older women, and he resigned himself to it, about to excuse himself gracefully, when his formidable instincts came into play.

"You were watching me?" he said instead. Dangerous, of course, but it was probably only the preliminaries of flirtation. She was a beautiful woman, but not his type. His type had suddenly become serene, leggy blondes. "Should I be flattered?"

She laughed. "Not particularly. You remind me of someone, and I can't figure out who it is."

It was an old ploy, and if he was lucky she was just engaging in a little clumsy flirtation. He wasn't feeling particularly lucky. "Can't help you there, Miss...?"

"Mrs." she said. "Mrs. Patrick Blackheart. You can call me Ferris."

He didn't even blink. She was watching him closely, as if she expected him to react, but he simply took her hand in his, resisting the impulse to bring it to his lips like a European gentleman. So this was his father's wife. He had good taste in women, Michael had to admit. And if he were a different sort of man he'd take a few hours to exact the perfect kind of pleasurable revenge on the man who'd abandoned him and his mother, by using all his practiced charm on the woman in front of him. He didn't doubt he could manage it—he'd never yet failed when he'd decided to seduce someone. Ferris Blackheart might be a challenge, but he could manage it, cuckolding his father quite nicely. It was momentarily tempting.

She disengaged her hand, giving him a wry smile. "Don't look at me like that—I'm old enough to be your mother," she chided him. "I was just trying to figure out where I'd seen you before."

"Maybe I just have one of those ordinary faces," he suggested.

"Oh, no, my boy. There's nothing the slightest bit ordinary about you. I saw you with Isabel earlier. What do you think of her?"

Michael resisted the impulse to look over his shoulder. "Very nice," he murmured.

"We're hoping to hire her for Blackheart, Incorporated. I'm afraid none of us are particularly well organized, and she has such a delightful sense of serenity about her. She's quite wasted on a poisonous little dweeb like Bill Helms."

"Wasted on him?" Blackheart echoed. "I didn't realize her relationship with him went beyond work."

"Oh, I don't think it does. Though you could always ask her."

"Mrs. Blackheart…"

"Call me Ferris. Everyone does except my husband, and he likes to be different. And you are?"

"Michael," he said. He'd given up any notion that she might be looking for a quick tumble. She might not have even the faintest suspicion of who he was, but she was smart enough to figure it out if he gave her even half a chance.

"Michael what?"

"Just Michael." He was a man who liked danger, who craved adrenaline, or had been for most of his life. "Would you care to dance, Mrs. Blackheart?"

She shook her head, smiling, though her eyes were troubled. "I think you'd be happier dancing with Isabel, Just Michael. She's over by the Monet, being bored to death by George Martin. Go rescue her."

She was dismissing him, and he ought to be suspicious. He was suspicious, but at the same time he'd turned and caught a glimpse of Isabel, looking just slightly desperate as an elderly man shouted in her ear.

"Then we'll dance later, you and I," he said lightly.

"Oh, we most definitely will," she replied.

He could feel her eyes on him as he threaded his way through the crowded reception, but when he glanced back he couldn't see her, and he told himself it was his imagination. Maybe he was getting rusty—

he'd been in jail in France for two seemingly endless years, and since he'd gotten out he hadn't stolen a thing. Uncle Felix said he was the most gifted thief of his generation, but gifts could vanish, talents could fade. And the fact of the matter was, his heart wasn't in it.

Too late to change his mind. Everything was in place, and he'd go ahead according to plan. The reception would be over at midnight—that gave him three more hours to while away his time sipping ginger ale and mentally counting his take. Three more hours to avoid Mrs. Patrick Blackheart and flirt with Isabel.

It was a dirty job, but he was more than happy to do it. He came up beside Isabel, and she turned, startled.

"I didn't even realize you were there."

"I'm very light on my feet," he said. "Dance with me."

She looked at the boring old man who'd been monopolizing her. "Oh, I can't..."

"Of course you can, sugar," the old man wheezed. "Let your boyfriend take you for a whirl. At my age a whiskey and soda will make up for the loss of your charming company."

"You're very sweet, Mr. Martin," she was saying, but Michael had already put his hand under her arm and was drawing her away, coolly determined.

"That was rude," she said breathlessly.

He turned and pulled her into his arms, and she fell against him, startled, staring at him in a kind of wary delight. ''I am rude,'' he said. ''When I want my own way.''

''And what's your own way?''

''Dance with me,'' he said, sliding his arm around her waist and pulling her into the music.

And she came with him, no longer fighting, her body fluid and soft and perfect against his, and he closed his eyes, breathing in the scent of her perfume, and wondered what she'd do when she found out he'd robbed her boss blind.

It didn't matter. All that mattered was this moment, their bodies moving against each other, the music soft and insistent, her skin flushed, her eyes wary, her mouth tremulous, and he wondered what would happen if he leaned down and kissed her, in front of everyone.

He wouldn't. He was being bad enough, flirting with her, dancing with her, holding her. He was here on a job, and he needed to concentrate on that, not on Isabel's creamy skin and the way her body fit against his.

Tomorrow she'd hate him, and with good reason. He didn't need to give her any more cause. No matter how desperately he wanted to.

No, for now he'd simply hold her, dance with her, closing his eyes and pretending it was another time, another night, and he wasn't the best living jewel thief in the world.

Just for a few moments he could give himself this pleasure. It wouldn't come again.

Chapter Three

Isabel Linden was a calm, unemotional, practical creature, who prided herself on her sense of order and responsibility. So what the hell was she doing, dancing with a perfect stranger, ignoring her duties? It didn't matter that she was going to quit Bill Helms's employ, it didn't matter that the security was in the capable hands of Blackheart, Inc. and the social aspects were controlled by Southworth's impressive staff. It didn't matter that Bill Helms had, for a change, stopped looking at her. She still had her own sense of duty, which seemed to have been shot to hell the moment Michael Blackheart pulled her into his arms.

To be truthful, it had probably happened the first moment she looked into his brown eyes, though she'd done her best to ignore the strange pull he had for her. But once he held her in his arms, once they started dancing, her last ounce of common sense vanished, and she'd simply closed her eyes and given in, embracing impracticality as her hands touched him.

The small dance band was one of the best in the Bay Area, and Isabel had gone to a great deal of trouble to hire them. Right about now she should be regretting it. They played dance tunes from the twenties and thirties, Parisian torch songs, and when they moved into a slow, sinuous blues Michael simply pulled Isabel up tighter against his body as they danced.

She could feel his erection, and she didn't care. He could probably feel her nipples through her silver, glittery dress. She was so turned on she could have grabbed his hand and dragged him off into the bushes, and she didn't care who was watching.

Their heads were so close, and all she would have had to do was turn, just a fraction of an inch, and their mouths would have met. She stopped herself, struggling for some last vestige of self-control. She might have temporarily lost her mind, but she hadn't lost her sense of self-preservation.

She pulled away, just a fraction of an inch, and looked up at him. "I didn't know dancing could be so...stimulating."

He laughed. "Maybe you just haven't had the right partner?"

"And you're the right partner?"

"What do you think?"

She couldn't deny it—she prided herself on being brutally honest. Of course, she prided herself on being responsible and in control, and those two attributes seemed to have deserted her. "It always seemed to be just a variant of foreplay,'' she said, trying to be offhand.

''And what's wrong with foreplay?''

So much for trying to be breezy, she thought. Why the hell had she brought up the subject of sex when her aroused body was pressed up against his? Hell, how could she help but bring it up?

''Nothing, I suppose. If you know what you're doing.''

''I always know what I'm doing,'' Michael said, tucking her head against his shoulder.

She stayed that way for a little while, still thinking about it. ''I'm not going to sleep with you tonight,'' she said after a moment, not lifting her head. At first he didn't say anything, and she wondered if he'd heard her, or if her voice had been too muffled against his warm, hard chest.

''I know you're not,'' he said finally. ''But it's not that you don't want to. You're just not that kind of a girl, right? You don't jump into bed with strangers, you don't fall in love at first sight, you don't risk everything for a perfect moment of passion.''

''No,'' she said. ''I don't.'' She half expected him to release her, but instead he pulled her back with a sexy little sigh.

''Too bad,'' he murmured. ''I'll just have to make do with foreplay.''

He was good, he was very good. Before she knew what he was doing he'd moved her through the crowds, into the darkness at the edge of the huge room. In a place filled with people and security he found a small, dark corner that was completely unobserved, pushed her up against the wall and kissed her.

Love at first sight. The words ran through her brain like a taunting litany. Isabel wasn't quite sure she believed in love, much less at first sight. But then right then she wasn't sure she knew anything at all, but the taste of his mouth on hers.

He knew how to kiss as well as dance. His mouth was a slow seduction, a deep, consensual plunder of hers, and she closed her eyes, shutting out the lights and the noise and even the sight of him, letting herself slide into the astonishing delight of his hungry mouth. His hands were moving down her sides, catching her hips and pulling her up against him, and she wondered if she could come just from kissing him, just from feeling him through her skimpy dress. Maybe she'd been celibate too long. Maybe she'd been too wise, too careful, and now it was all backfiring and she was off in the corner, necking with a gorgeous stranger when she should be working…

"Stop thinking," he growled in her ear. "No one can see us."

"I don't care about other people," she said, but her voice came out breathless, sexy. "I shouldn't be doing this."

He kissed her mouth, a slow, savoring kiss, then moved his lips to the soft spot beside her ear. "Why not?" he whispered.

"I have a job…"

"You're quitting."

"I don't know you."

"We've been introduced."

"I don't want..."

"Yes, you do," he said. In another man that would have been overbearing, obnoxious, deserving of a slap or at least a shove. With Michael it was simply the truth.

"Yes, I do," she agreed. And she slid her arms around his neck and kissed him back, ready to lose herself completely.

She wasn't expecting him to freeze. And then she heard Johnson's expressionless voice. "Miss Linden? Mr. Helms is looking for you."

She wondered for a brief, cowardly moment whether she could just hide behind his body. He was taller than she was, and out there in the darkened corridor Johnson couldn't be sure it was really her, wrapped around a total stranger.

Except for her silver dress. And Johnson didn't make mistakes—he was more robot than man.

Michael was moving, shielding her, so she pushed against him gently, and he backed away without a word. She smoothed her dress down over her body, wishing to hell that Johnson had showed up five minutes earlier or an hour later, and summoned her usual calm efficiency. "Of course, Johnson. Is something wrong?"

There was no censure in Johnson's colorless eyes, but then, the man had never expressed an emotion in all the time Isabel had known him. "No, ma'am. He just wanted me to find you."

If only she'd had the sense to quit that morning. But it was better late than never. She'd go with Johnson, quietly give Helms her notice, and then come

back to find Michael Blackheart again. And maybe
all her rules would be shot to hell, because maybe she
did believe in love at first sight after all.

11:00 p.m.

MICHAEL WATCHED HER GO, and he breathed a sigh
of mingled regret and relief. He still couldn't quite
believe it—he'd been ready to drop everything, ignore
the elaborate plans he'd made, abandon the job midstream, if she'd just come with him.

He'd been right all along—this was no longer his
business, his time. He'd pulled off some of the most
creative, daring heists in recent years, he'd done his
time in a French prison, and he was ready to get on
with life. He didn't need this last score, he didn't need
revenge against an absent father, he didn't even give
a damn about Bill Helms getting away with stolen
Nazi treasure. The war had been over for more than
half a century—time healed, and for all he knew Bill
Helms's neo-Nazi sympathies could have been part of
his uncle's paranoia. If Isabel Linden had agreed to
come back to his hotel room with him he would have
taken her, he would have taken her anywhere she was
willing to go, and to hell with the heist of the new
century.

But fate had stepped in in the shape of one of
Helms's Aryan bodyguards, and Michael had no
choice but to shrug and get on with his plans. At
midnight the party would end, the guests would de-
part, and the fabulous Helms treasure would be

packed up and driven back to Southworth's auction house for tomorrow night's event.

But they weren't going to arrive at their destination. He was going to take them, and the memory of Isabel's sweet mouth, and he would live with his regret.

And the substantial amount of money he'd get from fencing Helms's treasure. Surely that would calm any number of second thoughts. Wouldn't it?

Isabel was just vanishing into the crowds of people, surrounded by Helms's little army. He had a sudden, unpleasant fantasy—she looked like she was being carted away by Nazis. Ridiculous, since she was as tall and blond as any of Bill Helms's hand-picked bodyguards. Which brought him to another question—why was everyone who surrounded Bill Helms so aggressively Aryan? Was there more to his uncle's neo-Nazi paranoia than he'd first thought?

She had a beautiful back, Michael thought. The silvery dress caressed her body. Slid down her back, and he already knew she wasn't wearing a bra. He would have wanted to spend more time with that back of hers, with the front, upside down, anyway he could have her.

But duty, in the shape of grand theft, called, and he wasn't about to walk away for something as ephemeral as a slender back.

He glanced at his stolen Rolex. One more hour, and he'd let things slide. He'd taken it on his very first job, fifteen years ago, and despite the fact that a good Rolex should live forever, it was starting to lose time, and no jeweler had been able to fix it. Sooner or later it was going to stop entirely. He could only hope it wouldn't happen tonight.

Time was running out. He had one more thing to accomplish before the reception was officially over and he put things in motion.

He wanted to meet his father.

JOHN PATRICK BLACKHEART should have been enjoying the fruits of his labors. The Helms reception was going perfectly, his small, select staff working well with Southworth's cadre of security and perhaps a little less well with Helms's security staff. In one hour the last guest would be shooed from the place, the immense treasure would be loaded into an obscure-looking rental van and be driven the long way back to Southworth's auction rooms, while the official Southworth van would be loaded with boxes of catering equipment and driven boldly to its destination. Once the van arrived at Southworth his concerns were finished and done with, and Blackheart, Inc. would pocket a very nice piece of change.

Not that they were in particular need of income. Patrick had been considering cutting back on his jobs, rather than taking on more, and in fact he'd been turning more and more jobs over to his partner, Trace Walker. He'd been working hard for more than seventeen years, and he wanted a break. Without meaning to he'd become a workaholic, and he was tired of it all. He wanted to enjoy his children while they were still young, he wanted to enjoy his wife. If she was in the mood to let him.

He couldn't figure out what the hell had gotten into

her. She'd come with him to the reception, looking absolutely gorgeous, and as far as he could tell she'd been having a great time. The kids were bunked down at their uncle Trace's, and he had every intention of taking her back to their hotel room, plying her with champagne and cannoli, and making love to her on the thick Persian carpet in front of the fireplace. And then on the king-size bed. And then maybe in the Jacuzzi. Or on the desk. Or both.

It had been too damned long since they'd had a night alone, since they'd been able to really cut loose. He loved his children passionately, but at thirteen and eleven they seemed to be so...there. He'd been planning this night for a long time, and now it looked as if Francesca was going to make him sleep on the sofa, for no reason he could possibly imagine.

She'd stormed up to him an hour ago, her green eyes glinting sparks, her magnificent chest heaving. "You son of a bitch," she'd said in a bitter undertone.

Fortunately he'd moved away from the industrialist who was trying to get him to take on a new job. "I beg your pardon?"

"Don't give me that wide-eyed innocent crap," she'd snarled.

"Francesca..."

"And don't call me that. It's Ferris to you."

That was when he'd known he was in real trouble. "Darling," he'd begun, but she'd cut him off.

"You're a lousy father and a lousy human being," she said.

The "lousy father" hit hard, as she knew it would,

but he only blinked. As a matter of fact he was a very good father to Tim and Kate, and they both knew it. "Yeah," he said lazily, "but I'm a great thief and hell on wheels in bed."

"You think this is funny?" She really was outraged.

He shrugged. "Until I know what got your knickers in a twist I can't take it too seriously. We were necking on our way over here, now I'm some kind of serial killer. Do you want to explain?"

"Why don't you ask your son?" she said bitterly. And turning on her heel, she stalked away from him.

He allowed himself a moment to admire her progress. She'd filled out nicely during their fifteen years of generally blissful marriage. She thought she was too fat, of course, and nothing he could say would convince her otherwise, though usually actions spoke louder than words. And he had intended this to be a very active night, until Francesca decided to pitch a fit.

He moved out of the ballroom to a quiet corner and flipped open his cell phone. Trace's wife, Kate, answered on the second ring, sounding harried.

"Is everything okay?" Blackheart had asked, not betraying his sudden prickle of panic. If something had happened to Tim, Trace would have called him immediately, and the cell phone had been on all night. But Francesca didn't usually have a fit over nothing.

"The boys are watching some stupid action movie and behaving like children."

"They are children, Kate," he said patiently.

"Trace isn't. The moment Tim comes over he regresses. I'm making him pick up the popcorn they're throwing." She sounded her usual disgruntled self— Kate enjoyed complaining. Blackheart knew perfectly well she was devoted to her husband, to Tim and Kate, and to him and Ferris. She just liked to bitch. "So what's the problem?" she continued. "You suddenly don't trust us to take care of your children? We have three of our own and we haven't managed to break them yet."

"Just thought I'd check in," Blackheart said easily.

"Yeah, sure. Tell you what—you can clean up the spilled popcorn," she snapped.

"Give the kids a kiss for me."

"Enjoy your night with Ferris."

Yeah, right, Blackheart thought, ending the call. She wasn't going to let him come within ten feet of her until he found out what was bothering her. Some stupid misunderstanding, but she didn't seem like she was in the mood to listen.

He hadn't seen more than her back in the last hour—she definitely wasn't in the mood to explain what had set her off. In the meantime he concentrated on the job at hand—though things were well under control. At this point his presence was merely window dressing. The main part of the job had already been accomplished, and he hired the kind of people who knew how to make things run smoothly.

He glanced over at Bill Helms. He was surrounded by his small army of bodyguards. Blackheart couldn't figure out why Helms thought he was so important that he needed that kind of protection. Granted, he was rich as sin, but kidnapping a man like Helms wasn't the most lucrative scam someone could run. Better to go after something that mattered to the billionaire.

Like that leggy blonde. Isabel Linden had been responsible for most of the arrangements, and she'd seemed smart, sensible beneath her very decorative surface. She reminded him a bit of Francesca, though probably without the temper. Even from across the room Blackheart could see Helms practically drooling over Isabel. He knew body language well enough to read her response, even from a distance. She thought Helms was a toad.

Well, he was. A self-important little prick who thought he could buy anything. In fact, he probably could. But in the future he wouldn't be buying Blackheart, Inc. Dealing with Isabel had been fine, dealing with Henry Johnson and his Greek chorus had been a pain in the butt. In the future, Helms could handle things himself.

In the future. He just wished these people would start leaving so he could get the job done and get his wife to start explaining what set her off. The sooner he found out what had made her so pissed the sooner he'd be able to charm her out of her foul mood. And finish the night the way he'd planned.

He glanced around the ballroom. He had a strange prickling at the back of his neck, an itching between his shoulder blades, a roiling tension in his gut. Maybe it was caused by something as simple as having his wife mad at him, but he didn't think so.

Something wasn't right. He could feel it in his blood and bones and skin, his formidable instincts screaming at him. Something was going down, and he was going to have to stop it.

And Francesca was going to have to wait until later.

Chapter Four

Midnight

So much for Bill Helms getting over his ill-advised passion for her, Isabel thought irritably. He was staring up at her as if he was an alley cat and she was fresh mackerel. For some reason he didn't even seem to mind that she towered over him in her high heels, a deliberate move on her part. She plastered a polite smile to her freshly kissed mouth, and wondered where Michael Blackheart had disappeared to.

"It's going well, don't you think?" Helms said. His eyes were glistening behind his glasses. He was milky pale, freckled and surprisingly unappealling. Isabel managed an encouraging smile.

"Very well. Southworth has done an excellent job, and I have complete faith in Blackheart, Inc.," she said. Helms's little cadre of bodyguards had faded back, out of earshot but not out of reach, and she wondered why he'd thought it necessary to send his private army for her.

"Not just Southworth," he said smoothly. "You've

outdone yourself, Isabel. And I'm not a man who fails to reward loyalty.''

Loyalty had nothing to do with it. "It's my job, Mr. Helms," she said.

"Bill," he corrected. "I've told you to call me Bill.''

That was the last thing she wanted. The first thing she wanted was to be back in Michael Blackheart's arms. "Bill," she said with a tight smile.

"And I've got something for you. A little token of my appreciation," he murmured. "I think things are running well enough that you could take a few moments away."

"I don't think I ought to…"

"Everything went smoothly while you were dancing with that man. Even when you disappeared with him. Who was he, by the way? I don't remember anyone of his description being on the guest list.''

"The guest list was huge, vetted by Southworth and Blackheart, Inc. There's no way you could personally know everyone," she said, suddenly uneasy.

"But I make it my business to know everyone and everything that could possibly affect me. That's how I got where I am today. Who was he?''

There was absolutely no reason why she shouldn't tell him. "Actually I don't think I got his name. John something."

"That's not like you, Isabel. I've always admired your attention to details." He put his soft hand under her arm and drew her out of the crowded room. She couldn't very well resist—it would cause a scene, and Isabel hated scenes. Besides, Henry Johnson and his tuxedoed friends had closed ranks, following them. She looked out over their heads into the crowd, searching for Michael, but there was no sign of him.

"The job's almost done," she said. "I decided to relax my standards for a bit. Where are we going?"

"It's a surprise," Helms said. "And just because tonight's almost finished with doesn't mean the job is over. We can accomplish wonderful things together, Isabel. I can sense it."

She wasn't going to accomplish a damned thing with him, and it didn't matter if he really was the third richest man in the entire universe. She considered yanking free, but with the phalanx of men behind her she wouldn't get far. Not that they'd physically stop her, of course. She was getting paranoid.

A moment later he swept her into a small salon. There was a bucket of ice with a bottle of champagne in it, two crystal flutes and a huge white box on the French settee. Johnson closed the door behind them, sealing them alone in the little room, doubtless keeping guard.

"I had this brought from my wine cellar especially for you, Isabel." Helms had released her arm and gone to pour the champagne. "I realize I've been inattentive, but this auction has taken up a great deal of my time. I want to make it up to you."

"Inattentive?" she echoed, taking the champagne flute from him absently. "You're my boss. I work for you. There's no reason you should pay me the slightest bit of attention as long as you've been satisfied with my performance."

"But we could do so much more together. I've

been watching you, Isabel. You're everything I most admire in a woman, both spiritually and…er…physically. I want us to work together even more closely in the future.''

Tell him, she ordered herself. Tell him you quit, tonight, and that you never want him to put his soft, damp hands on you again. She cleared her throat. ''Mr. Helms…''

''Bill,'' he corrected, and clinked the crystal flute against hers. ''To us.''

She didn't need to look at the label of the champagne to know it would probably be the best she'd ever had, and she had a definite weakness for champagne. She set the glass down on the table. ''I don't think socializing is a very good idea, under the circumstances. I should get back.''

A petulant expression darkened his bland eyes for a moment, and then he smiled. ''You haven't seen your present yet.''

''I don't need a present. You pay me extraordinarily well.''

He was ignoring her protests, of course. Bill Helms had a habit of ignoring anything he wanted to, and he got away with it. He turned and picked up the huge box. It was almost as big as he was, and he staggered a bit before handing it to her. ''For you, Isabel. A token of my sincere…affection.''

It was more bulky than heavy, and she had no choice but to sit down on one of the delicate, uncomfortable settees. She was a woman who liked oversized, overstuffed furniture, and if Helms thought he was going to manage a romantic rendezvous on one of these hard little settees then he overestimated the lure of his fortune.

She didn't recognize the name on the huge white box. "Open it," he insisted. "I had it custom-made for you."

She untied the white satin ribbon, lifted off the top of the box and stared down in dismay. It was a mass of soft, white fur. She just stared at it in horror.

"Try it on," Helms said gaily, pulling it out of the box. It was a full-length fur coat, made out of some poor, fuzzy white animal, and it was rich, luxurious and horrible.

"I'm a vegetarian," she said flatly.

"I'm not asking you to eat it," Helms said in an irritable voice, some of his pleasure fading. "It's ermine. I had it custom-made for your height. It'll look glorious on you."

"You had those baby animals killed especially for me?" she said.

He shoved the coat into her arms. The fur was soft, warm, extraordinarily beautiful, but it belonged on the backs on its original owners, not hers.

"They weren't babies, they were fully grown, and they were bred for that purpose. Don't be naive, Isabel. In this world there are the strong and the weak, the takers and the givers. Weaselly little rodents were put on this earth to provide beautiful warm coats for beautiful, cold women. Not that you're cold. Or if you are, just enough to make it a challenge."

He was smirking at her. Isabel shoved the box off her lap and rose, tossing the heavy coat onto the settee. "Maybe weasely little rodents were put on this earth to be protected from people like you."

Helms shook his head. "It's dog eat dog, Isabel. Just be glad you're part of the master race."

"The what?" Her voice rose in a controlled shriek.

For the first time Bill Helms looked flustered. "I mean the ruling class. The haves, as opposed to the have-nots. We're the people who run this country, Isabel. We have the wisdom, the power, the genetics…"

"Genetics?" she echoed, no longer making any attempt to behave herself. "Master race? What kind of neo-Nazi fascist creep are you?"

She wasn't particularly interested in whether she offended him or not, but she was unprepared for his reaction. Suddenly he was as grim and cold as ice, no longer the annoying, rich little dweeb with his small army of bodyguards. For the first time she could understand the tenacity that had led to his amassing an obscene fortune.

"You've been spying," he said, his voice soft and dangerous. "I should have known you couldn't keep that perfect, pretty little nose out of things that don't concern you. I thought I kept you busy, but I must have underestimated you. What interests me is why you haven't done anything about it."

She didn't bother hiding her incredulous reaction. "What the hell are you talking about?" she said. "Are you completely out of your mind? I don't want your bloodstained coat, I don't want your champagne, I don't want your attentions and I don't want your stinking job. I quit." She spun on her heel and headed for the door, half afraid she'd find it locked. She felt odd, disoriented, as if she were in some strange Victorian melodrama with Bill Helms twirling an oily mustache. But the door opened beneath her touch, and she flung it open, ready to stalk away.

But Henry Johnson, with his brush-cut blond hair, blocked her exit, his ice-blue eyes cold and expressionless. "Is there a problem, sir?" he asked in his emotionless voice.

"I'm afraid I've been mistaken in Miss Linden," Helms said. "She's been prying into things that don't concern her, and I'm very much afraid she's become an inconvenience."

She turned back to look at Helms, irritation and fear warring for control. "I have no idea what you're talking about. All I know is you'd better let me leave or I'll scream so loud the alarm system will seem like a lullaby."

"You heard her, George," Helms said softly. "She leaves us no choice."

She didn't even have time to turn back. The tiny stinging sensation at the base of her neck was the last thing she remembered, and as she fell to the floor her eyes focused on the white fur coat. Maybe she should have taken the damned thing.

And then everything went black.

MICHAEL DIDN'T SEE ISABEL again, and he told himself it was just as well. He'd already let himself get far too distracted from the job at hand. In a few days, he'd be back in Europe, celebrating the success of his final job, and Isabel would be a bittersweet memory, one he'd think of fondly. A few days, maybe a few weeks at the most. Months if he was really unlucky.

Or he could be like his uncle Felix, who had fallen in love with his aunt Margot and never looked at another woman in the last sixty-seven years, even through two decades of being widowed.

With luck he didn't take after that side of the family. He'd be much happier to be like his father, who walked out of women's lives and never thought twice about them, even when they were carrying a child.

No, scratch that. He'd rather not care at all, one way or the other. He'd been working on it, thought he'd made some progress, until he laid eyes on Isabel Linden and had been half tempted to forget everything but her deep, blue eyes.

His one regret was that he hadn't managed to set eyes on his long-lost father. It would have been amusing to saunter up to him, maybe discuss the relative value of Helms's long-lost Nazi treasure, and all the time Patrick Blackheart would wonder why he looked so familiar, who he reminded him of. Then again, maybe he wouldn't remind him of anyone at all. And why the hell should Michael care, for that matter? He was there to give Blackheart, Inc. a black eye. His father didn't have to know who delivered the coup de grâce.

He slipped out of the ballroom with the chattering crowds, secure in the knowledge that no one would notice him. Only he didn't wander toward a taxi, or a waiting limo, or even go for a midnight stroll as some of his fellow revelers were doing. Keeping his pace leisurely, he headed straight back to his room, ignoring the pang of regret that he was alone and sticking to business. When he left the room, forty-five minutes later, no one would recognize him as the elegant young gentleman who'd set off the burglar alarms.

Blackheart, Inc.'s security plan was elegant and simple, and against most thieves it would have been effective. Once the reception room was cleared, the art treasures would be packed into heavy wooden crates and loaded into Southworth's armored truck for delivery to that venerable establishment's front door. In the meantime, the catering supplies were packed in cheap cardboard and moved into one of those anonymous rental trucks for return to the catering establishment. The security guards would handle the priceless treasures, the catering staff would handle the loading of the rental truck and then two of Southworth's lesser employees would see to their delivery.

Except that the rental truck wouldn't be going to Tucker by the Bay, but instead to the hidden side entrance of Southworth's auction house. The cheap cardboard boxes would be filled with Renoir and Monet and Lalique and Fabergé, the custom wooden crates would hold cheap crystal and silver plate. And not even the drivers would know.

Though, in this case, the driver would know, Michael thought, adjusting his baseball cap on his head and unfastening the top button of his black jean jacket. Tucker by the Bay Catering Institute was emblazoned on the back of the jacket, and the bill of the cap shaded his face. He'd transformed his gait into an ambling sort of pace, and before anyone noticed his sudden appearance at the loading dock he'd already scooped up a cardboard box of priceless treasures marked flatware and carried it to the truck.

Helms's little cadre of bodyguards were watching, making no effort to help the catering staff. They were all practically identical, from their crew-cut blond hair to their expressionless eyes and gym-toned bodies. Where was Isabel? he wondered as he reached for another crate, brushing past a fellow worker who didn't even notice that he'd just arrived. Was she flirting with Bill Helms, drinking champagne and laughing? Forgetting about the slow dance and the slower kisses?

"You there!" One of Helms's men was calling to him, and he considered ignoring the voice. He'd already run into the same man twice tonight, when he'd deliberately tripped the alarms and when they'd taken Isabel away. Johnson, Isabel had called him.

Michael stopped, looking up into the icy eyes with as much California laid-back disdain as he could. "I don't remember you in the kitchens," Johnson said. Clearly not remembering him from anyplace else.

"I'm part of the cleanup crew, man," Michael said lazily. "You want to load silverware in my place, feel free."

Johnson peered at him suspiciously, not quite satisfied. Then he shrugged. "Never mind. We're almost finished—you can go home now."

"Who's going to drive the van back?" He already knew they'd planned to send one of Blackheart's workers, but none of them seemed to be anywhere around. Only the Boys from Brazil.

"That's not your concern. Arrangements have been made with your company."

By this time the other members of the kitchen staff had moved away, unsuspicious and glad of an early evening. Michael summoned up a cocky grin. "Suit yourself," he said. "I got better things to do." They watched him as he left. He took his time, but he could feel those identical sets of cold blue eyes digging into his back. He could only be glad that Helms had decided to trust his own men rather than Blackheart's. Brawn was always easier to circumvent than brain, and none of Bill Helms's omnipresent bodyguard seemed overburdened with intellect.

He slipped into the front seat of the truck, waiting patiently. He couldn't see what they were doing, but apparently they had one more thing to load into the truck before they took off, and he leaned against the seat, whistling softly to himself. The keys were in the ignition—an added bonus, but he would have made do without them quite easily. He never had even the faintest doubt that his plan would work. Sheer audacity was half the battle in successful burglary.

He heard the backdoors of the truck slam shut, the grinding of the locks. He glanced in the rearview mirror at the two men left standing there by the loading dock. They were probably armed and dangerous, and Michael made it a practice never to carry a gun. He knew how to use one, but they gave him the creeps. If the situation came when he couldn't outthink some gun-toting thug, then he deserved to be shot.

He'd planned on simply blending in as part of the catering crew, and going from there, but things were looking both more complicated and a great deal simpler. He'd already covered his tracks—it had been a simple matter to sabotage Blackheart's surveillance van with the cute little technological toy supplied by his uncle Felix. It was a magnetic system that worked somewhat along the lines of an MRI, and its short bursts of power were phenomenal and almost untraceable. He only hoped there wasn't a video rental store within three blocks—their stock would be wiped clean as well.

It was the least of his problems. With the catering crew dismissed, that simply left the drivers. And with those drivers at the back end of the truck and Michael in the cab with the keys at hand, the answer was simple. No need to bother with any subterfuge once they got to Southworth's loading bay. The planned diversion could go off and no one would care, since this truck was never going to make it across town.

He leaned forward, turned the key, and the engine roared to life. He had the last, satisfying glimpse of Helms's goons running after him as he sped away from the back entrance, and sure enough, they'd pulled guns out of their custom-made tuxedoes. He resisted the impulse to duck as bullets sprayed past him, one shattering the driver's side window. With a squeal of tires he was around the corner, out into the midnight streets of San Francisco, and Helms's gun-toting goons were left in the dust.

In the back of his anonymous rental truck was millions upon millions of dollars worth of stolen Nazi treasure. Worth a hell of a lot more than Isabel Linden's sweet mouth, though he could have wished he had both.

But life was seldom as convenient as that, and besides, this whole thing had been embarrassingly easy for a final heist. All he had to do was get the truck safely away, into the abandoned warehouse he'd already earmarked, before Helms's men could come after him. They'd have to call the police, or it would look suspicious.

But Michael Blackheart was more than a match for fascist bodyguards and the world's finest police forces. He was more than a match for his esteemed father, the greatest living cat burglar in the world.

He was going to get away with it. Not that he'd ever doubted whether he would or not. He was going to go back home with money, revenge and his family's honor assuaged.

And the memory of Isabel Linden to keep him up at nights.

Chapter Five

1:00 a.m.

Bill Helms was foaming at the mouth. Patrick Blackheart watched his approach with a wary eye. He should have listened to his wife—she'd warned him against getting mixed up with Helms. Of course, she'd had no excuse other than her formidable instincts, and that hadn't been enough reason to turn down a high-profile, lucrative contract. He should have listened to her. This had been nothing but a pain in the butt since the very beginning, with Helms being officious, secretive, forcing Blackheart, Inc. to go through his cadre of military-style middlemen. The only useful thing about the whole experience was Isabel Linden, and Francesca had already said she was going to hire her away from Helms.

The job was over—gone off without a hitch. At the last minute Helms's men had taken over the final stage of loading and delivering the Norenheld Treasure back to Southworth's, over Patrick's strenuous objections, but it was no longer his responsibility.

There was nothing to do but find out where his furious wife was, beguile her into forgiving him for whatever imagined transgression he'd committed, and send his bill to Bill Helms.

Francesca was waiting for him by the ballroom doorway, her wrap around her shoulders, and he could tell by the way she held her body that she wasn't in a forgiving mood. Helms was bearing down on him, flanked by his goons, and Patrick had the feeling that the good evening was about to go terribly wrong.

"What the hell are you doing standing there?" Helms shrieked at him from halfway across the ballroom. "We've been robbed!"

The place was deserted except for the hotel crew breaking down the tables, and by their lack of reaction he guessed that few of them could speak English. He waited for Helms to get closer, then asked in his calm voice, "Did you call the police?"

It stopped Helms cold. "Not yet. I hired you to take care of security, and you screwed up! I'll have your license, I'll sue your butt…"

"You'd dismissed my services, Helms," Patrick said calmly. "You told me your men were capable of handling it from that point on. Clearly you were mistaken."

Helms cast a look of sheer rage at his stoic bodyguards. "It was on your watch…"

"Not anymore," he corrected him. "What happened?" Francesca had left her post by the door and was drifting closer, curious as always. Strange, but she didn't seem terribly surprised by the news.

"These idiots aren't even sure what happened.

They had just finished loading the rental truck when someone drove it away. Just up and stole the damned truck without these fools even realizing what was happening. They don't even know who was driving, though they think it was some member of the kitchen staff."

"I shot him," Henry Johnson said in his expressionless voice. "I know I hit him."

"Him? What did he look like?"

"I don't know. He was wearing a hat. He might have looked familiar."

"Very observant," Patrick said softly. "A man with a hat strolls up to a truck containing millions of dollars worth of art treasures and drives off under your nose. I think you're squat out of luck, Helms. Better call the police."

"That's the best you can offer?" Helms fumed. "You're the best in the business—that's why I hired you. Are you telling me you're ignoring your responsibilities?"

"My only responsibility is to clients who do as I tell them to do. I told you it would be safer if my people handled the transfer but you chose to do it your way."

By this time Helms was looking less furious and more panicked. "You have to find it for me, Blackheart!"

"Call the police."

"You don't understand—I don't want the publicity. I just want the treasure back, no questions asked."

"Can't help you there."

"Of course you can. That's why I hired you in the

first place, that's how you've built your reputation. You know how thieves think. I need you to find that rental truck, Blackheart, and the man who took it. Before word gets out that it's been stolen.''

"And the thief? If I find him, and I'm not saying that I have any intention of doing so, will you hand him over to the police?''

Helms shook his head. "We can handle it from there. I don't want you to interfere—just find out where it is. My men can take care of the situation much more effectively without involving the police or the courts.''

Patrick opened his mouth to suggest Helms perform an anatomically impossible act, when he realized his wife was beside him, slipping her arm through his. He looked down at her, but she didn't meet his gaze.

"We'll find the truck and the thief, Mr. Helms,'' she said.

"You'll find we can be very generous...'' Helms began, but Francesca cut him off.

"Part of the service, Mr. Helms,'' she said smoothly. "We'll be in touch shortly.'' Patrick didn't have any misapprehension about the gentle tug on his arm. If he'd resisted his dainty wife would have discreetly stomped on his foot.

"I just want you to tell me where it is,'' he said again, a touch of desperate menace in his voice. "I don't want you to go near the truck.''

"We'll be in touch,'' Francesca said in her soothing voice.

"I wonder why he's so desperate to keep us from

looking inside the truck,'' she muttered beneath her breath as they left the deserted ballroom. Patrick didn't say a word. After fifteen years of marriage he knew when to let his wife have the lead, and he was, as always, amused and curious as to see where it would take them.

Their first stop was the registration desk at the Carlyle. ''I've lost my key,'' she said sweetly. ''The name is Blackheart.''

Patrick was about to interrupt and tell her that he had the key to their room but he wisely fell silent when the clerk said, ''Which Blackheart would that be, madame? Mr. Michael Blackheart or Mr. Patrick Blackheart?''

Patrick didn't like the sudden sinking sensation in the pit of his stomach. Who the hell was Michael Blackheart? And why did his wife seem to know of his existence?

He had to wait until they got back in their own room—Francesca's talent at subterfuge didn't extend to getting the key to someone else's room. They rode up the elevator in silence, and by then she'd stepped away from him, clearly not wanting to touch him. He'd change her mind, of course. Once he figured out what the hell was going on.

He'd already taken off his coat and tie by the time they reached their room. He tossed them on the bed, taking only a brief moment to remember the better things he'd had planned for that bed, and shut the door behind him.

''Okay, spill. What the hell is going on, and who is Michael Blackheart?''

Francesca kicked off her high heels, dumped her shawl on the bed beside his jacket and glared at him out of her magnificent green eyes. "Your son, the thief," she said. "Isn't it obvious?"

"I only have one son, and he's eleven years old and sound asleep at Trace's house."

"Then obviously you haven't met Michael."

"And you have?"

"It took me the most ridiculously long amount of time to realize who he reminded me of. He's got blond hair, but he's got your cheekbones, your eyes, your build. He even walks like you."

"Francesca," he said patiently, "I have no other sons. Trust me."

"Not that you know of, maybe," she said. Clearly not appeased. "It's no excuse—you can't go around fathering children and then forgetting about them."

"I never knew about him in the first place!" he exploded. "If I even believe in his existence at all. What makes you think he could possibly be my son, apart from that fact that we share the same physical type?"

"The fact that once he heard my name he refused to tell me his last name. The fact that a high-profile robbery has been carried off under your nose by one man who fits the same description. He's inherited your looks, your talent and obviously a grudge against the father who abandoned him. Ergo, he's the thief. What I don't understand is why Helms is so reluctant to involve the police."

"I'm not buying this, Francesca."

"You don't want to find your son before Helms's

goons get to him? Fine. You go to Trace's house and take care of the children while he and I go looking for him.''

''You're beginning to piss me off, Ferris,'' he growled, using the name she hated.

''It's nothing compared to how I feel about you,'' she snapped back. ''How could you?''

He sighed. ''I told you, I didn't. What does this so-called son of mine look like? Convince me.''

''I can do more than that. The security cameras would have a photo of him. We can go downstairs and scan them...''

''You promised Helms an answer by noon. Do you have any idea how long it would take to go through those films?''

''He looks like a gypsy.''

Again, that sharp punch in the stomach. ''You said he was blond,'' he protested.

But Francesca knew him too well. ''That rings a bell, doesn't it, you son of a bitch. Who was she?''

He hesitated, still refusing to believe in the possibility. ''Long before your time, sweetheart. I was still a teenager. And she couldn't have gotten pregnant. If she had, her father would have killed me or we would have been married before the first trimester. There's no way...''

''The timing's right. He looks in his late twenties. Congratulations, Patrick Blackheart, it's a bouncing baby boy,'' Francesca said bitterly.

''So it's my fault if they never told me? If I never knew?''

''You should have made the effort to make sure

everything was all right. Even back then you would have known about condoms.''

''I was in jail, Francesca,'' he said finally. ''That's why they couldn't find me, couldn't come after me. I remember now. Elena and I spent the night together, and the next day I was picked up by the police. It was in Prague, and the police weren't very forthcoming as to who they had in their custody, why, or for how long. She probably thought I'd dropped off the face of the earth. Which in fact I had.''

''They didn't hold you forever. You could have gone to her when you got out...''

''I escaped, darling. I'm very good at getting out of tight places when I need to. And I didn't have any time for lingering farewells—I needed to get the hell out of that country as fast as I could. Besides, after two weeks surviving the hospitality of the Czech police I'd pretty much forgotten anything that had happened in the recent past.''

She shook her head. ''You don't get off so lightly.''

''I'm not getting off lightly at all. If you're right, and I have a grown son who's just pulled off a multi-million dollar robbery that I'm supposed to solve, then I'd say I'm paying for my sins. Why the hell did you tell Helms we'd find him?''

''Better we do than those goose-stepping goons. They'd kill him.''

''Don't be ridiculous. Bill Helms isn't some kind of gangster—he's a self-made millionaire and a...''

''He's an amoral creep. I don't trust him farther than I could throw him, and I didn't want to take this job in the first place. You should have listened to me.''

''But then we never would have found my supposed long-lost son, would we?'' he shot back.

She said nothing, staring at him. ''You still don't believe it, do you?''

''You're not leaving me much choice. Once I see him I'll know. He's probably some up-and-coming thief out to exploit a surface resemblance. Hell, I would have done the same thing in his place.''

''Yes, you would have. Which makes it even more likely that he's your...''

''Enough!'' he snapped. ''I need to think.''

''Think about what?''

''You told Helms we'd find him, right? And I have every intention of doing just that, just to prove to myself and to you that he's not related to me. Since we've got such a short time frame I can't afford to waste it. Be quiet and let me think.''

Instead of taking offense she nodded approvingly. ''I'll call some of your old buddies from the trade. They might have heard something. He'll have to have made some arrangements ahead of time. He couldn't just walk into a job this big totally unprepared.''

''You may not find much,'' he said. ''If he's like me, or anyone in the business, he's both careful and imaginative. He'd cover his tracks, and be ready to change plans midstream if it suits him.''

''You'll find him,'' she said, leaning over and brushing a kiss against his lips. ''I still love you, you know.''

He glanced up at her. "Are you ready to be the stepmother of a grown man?"

"As long as he's not in any hurry to give me grandchildren," she said. "There are limits to my maternal nature.

THE BASTARDS HAD MANAGED to hit him. He hadn't even noticed when the glass shattered beside him, too intent on getting as far away as fast as he could, but he could feel the cold stinging sensation in his arm, and even in the dim light of the truck's dashboard he could see the black ooze of blood on his jacket.

Only a graze, he told himself, cursing as he made a sharp turn. It hurt like hell but he wouldn't even need to avail himself of the underground medical resources that he knew he could find in any city of the world. The moment he got to his destination he could wash the damned thing and bandage it, and no one would be the wiser.

It wasn't the first time he'd been shot. With luck it would be the last. He was getting too old for this stuff. For the first time he felt none of the exhilaration, the adrenaline rush that usually buoyed him through the next twenty-four hours. As a matter of fact, he felt depressed, not triumphant. His instincts had told him it was past time to get out of the game, and he should have listened to them rather than Uncle Felix. In the end he'd never even come face-to-face with his so-called father. All he'd managed to do was run off with a great deal of expensive stuff that he'd fence for a tiny portion of its value, knowing he'd given a black eye to his father's company and a monkey wrench in the works of Bill Helms's possible neo-Nazi activities.

He wasn't sure it was worth it.

There were no sirens, which surprised him. He was still close enough to the Carlyle to hear if the police had been called in. He knew some of Helms's goons had come after him, but he could drive like the man he'd always supposed was his father, the Le Mans racer, and even with the unwieldy rental truck he could outmaneuver just about anyone or anything.

It took him fifteen minutes to get to the abandoned warehouse he'd chosen. If he'd gone straight there it would have taken less than five minutes on the empty streets of San Francisco, but he'd taken as many turns and twists as he dared. He left the truck running as he jumped out to drag open the door, cursing his arm as he did it. He drove through and closed it behind him, noticing at the last minute the drops of blood from his arm. He didn't have time to cover it up, and besides, it was off a dark alleyway. Bright lights and hi-tech equipment might pick it up, but if they got that far he was screwed anyway. He rubbed the marks with his foot, jumped back into the truck and drove into the cavernous belly of the abandoned warehouse.

When he'd gotten to the dark center of the place he turned off the engine, leaned back against the seat and closed his eyes, taking a few deep breaths. His arm stung like hell, a good sign that it was only a surface wound. His heart was steady, his pulses even—he didn't even get a decent rush from one of the biggest scores of his life. Definitely time to change careers.

He slid out of the cab of the truck and headed around to the back. The poor bastards hadn't even gotten around to locking it. Really, this whole thing was too easy, despite the fact that he'd been winged. He pulled off the baseball cap, shaking his hair free, and stripped off the bloody jeans jacket. The night was cool, but he didn't mind. He had a naturally high body temperature and he seldom got chilled—an advantage in his line of work.

Former line of work, he amended mentally, reaching for the clean bandanna that had been part of his getup and wrapping it around his upper arm. The blood had soaked into his Grateful Dead T-shirt, but the graze was shallow and essentially harmless. He'd be fine.

He yanked open the doors of the rental truck and peered into the darkness. It was kind of like Christmas morning, he thought grimly, except he didn't get to keep the presents. If he had his choice, he would have kept that pretty little Vermeer. And on a purely sentimental note, he would have held on to the Lalique music box with its pretty little melody. He would have liked to send it to Isabel anonymously, but unfortunately she struck him as the honest type, and she would have just given it back to Helms.

No, maybe he'd hold on to the box himself, a souvenir of his last, great heist, and when he looked at it he'd think of Isabel and what might have been.

He climbed up into the truck, reaching for the overhead light, when he noticed something unexpected back behind the boxes. White fur, and he wondered for a moment if a very large albino rat had crawled into the back. He moved closer, and he saw a woman's foot, clad in a silver sandal. It wasn't a particularly small foot—it had to belong to a tall woman who'd undoubtedly worn silver or white to the reception, and he didn't know whether to curse or laugh. He'd inadvertently run off with Isabel Linden, the greatest treasure of all.

And then he realized she wasn't moving.

Chapter Six

2:00 a.m.

Isabel was having the strangest dreams. Bill Helms was running around in a brown uniform, wearing a mustache that made him look strangely like Hitler, and he was shrieking in some incomprehensible language that she couldn't recognize. There were others milling around, and she was wrapped in something incredibly soft and warm and being carted around like a sack of potatoes. Very strange, and upsetting to her dignity, though she wasn't quite sure why she was worried about her dignity in the middle of this incredibly bizarre dream.

Michael Blackheart was there as well, except that he'd turned into a cross between a Deadhead and a pirate. His hair was long, and he was staring down at her, his elegant face dark with worry. He turned into a doctor, which was a great deal more soothing, considering that she was feeling very strange, but then she opened her eyes, to find herself in the middle of a dark, huge cavern, and Michael Blackheart was a pirate after all.

She was lying on something furry, and she didn't want to think about what it was. She stared up at Michael, trying to focus, trying to remember what happened.

"Where the hell am I?" she demanded in a voice that was barely more than a choked whisper.

The Pirate Blackheart didn't say anything. She sat up, moaning at the sudden wooziness that swept over her. "What's going on?" she tried again.

The Pirate had a red bandanna tied around his upper arm. Nicely muscular arm, she noticed dazedly. But then, she'd already discovered he was very strong.

And he wasn't answering her. She reached out, grabbed the Grateful Dead T-shirt in her fist and yanked him toward her, nose to nose. "I asked you a question," she said in the closest she could come to a snarl.

It wasn't very close. A small smile tugged at the corner of his mouth, and she was wondering whether she had the strength to hit him, when he finally spoke. "You've been drugged."

His English accent was much more pronounced. He must have had his hair tied back—she hadn't realized how long it was. And maybe he had worn that Dead T-shirt underneath his Armani tuxedo, but she didn't think so.

She was only able to sit up because she still had a firm grip on his T-shirt, and fortunately he did nothing to make her release him. "Why? Are you into drugging and raping women?"

"Hey, I didn't do it!" he protested. He'd slid his arm around her shoulders, supporting her, but she had no intention of releasing her stranglehold on the shirt. It was her one connection to reality. "Besides, I hate to be ungentlemanly, but you were more than willing to come with me anyway. I didn't have to resort to drugs."

"No," she said miserably, looking at his pirate face. "You didn't."

"So the question is, who drugged you and dumped you in the back of the truck, and why?"

"Truck? What truck?"

He didn't answer that one, either. She looked past his face, trying to focus, but it was only a cavernous darkness. "I think I need to lie down," she said.

He set her back gently, but she still hadn't let go of his T-shirt, and he didn't seem to be interested in making her. He simply leaned over her, patiently waiting.

But he was too distracting. The world was spinning too much for her to let go of him, but she closed her eyes, trying to blot out the strangeness, trying to regain some kind of control.

"Who are you?" she whispered. "Are you a pirate?"

There was a long hesitation, as if he were seriously considering her question. Finally he spoke. "Close," he said. "I'm a cat burglar."

She let go of his T-shirt and sank back on the fur.

"Cat burglar? You steal cats? Is that what I'm lying on?"

"I think you're still a little punchy from whatever Helms gave you. You're lying on a fur coat that probably cost more than the gross national product of some third world countries."

"Are you going to steal it?"

"I might."

She opened her eyes again. Even though she was no longer clinging to him he hadn't moved very far away, and in the mysterious darkness he was the only thing she could recognize.

"I don't wear fur."

"I'll keep that in mind. Where did you get it? Helms?"

Things were slowly coming into focus. "How did you guess?"

"He's the only one who could afford it. He's the only one with the manpower to drug you and dump you in the back of a panel truck, for that matter. What did you do to offend him?"

"Told him I didn't want the coat."

"That's a bit of an overreaction."

"I told him I didn't want him."

"He should have figured that out by now."

"And I told him he was a Nazi."

"Ouch!" Michael said. "Therein lies the problem. You hit a little too close to the bone."

Her eyes opened wider. "He really is a Nazi?"

"Most likely a neo-Nazi sympathizer. The entire Norenheld collection is made up of stolen art treasures from World War Two, according to my uncle, who has the sources to find out such things.''

"So you thought it would be okay to steal things that were already stolen?"

"It's what I do."

She stared at him in dismay. "And here I thought I'd found my soul mate," she said.

"Maybe you did."

"Go to hell." She sat up, brushing away his attempt at helping her. "If you don't tell me where we are I'm going to scream, very loudly."

"It won't do any good—there's no one within hearing distance. We're in an abandoned warehouse down by the waterfront, and not a soul knows we're here. So go ahead and scream."

"Are you going to kill me?"

"Not even tempted," he replied in a lazy voice. "You've been an inconvenience since the moment I laid eyes on you, but I can deal with unexpected complications."

"Obviously you were sucking up to me because you thought I could help you with access to the collection," she said bitterly.

"Obviously I was sucking up to you because I couldn't help myself, despite the fact that the only smart thing to do would have been to keep my distance."

She didn't bother to hide her suspicions. "You're telling me you were swept away by my charm and beauty?"

He cocked his head, watching her. "I don't think

so. I've never let charming and beautiful women distract me before. I think it's fate. Kismet.''

"Horse hockey," Isabel snapped. "Help me up.''

He rose, reaching a hand out to her, and she took it, letting him pull her to her feet. It wasn't such a good idea after all. For one thing, he was still holding onto her hand, which she found distracting and oddly comforting. For another, she was having a hard time maintaining her balance and the last thing she wanted was to fall into Michael Blackheart's arms.

But she was made of stern stuff, so she pulled her hand free, straightened her knees and tried not to sway. "What is this place?"

"A sort of a high-end chop shop," he said, moving away from her, obviously deciding she wasn't going to take a header. There was a long table near the van, the only piece of furniture she could see in the darkness, and he slid on top of it. "I was planning on breaking down the treasures, taking the paintings out of their frames, repacking the jewelry, and getting the stuff ready to store until I could arrange to sell it. It's too large a cache to get rid of easily. No one's going to come looking for it except Helms, and he's easy enough to deal with."

"So I can assume you really are related to Blackheart, and he's decided to get back in the business of robbery. Assuming he ever left it in the first place?''

Michael's smile was ironic. "Yes and no. As far as I know he's on the straight and narrow, but yes, he's my father. He just doesn't happen to care. Or maybe he doesn't even know it. It doesn't matter anymore. I did this on my own. It's what I do.''

"How enterprising." She took a step toward him, then realized she was wearing only one of her sandals. She had no idea where the other one was, and the cement floor of the old warehouse was cold beneath her feet, but she kicked it off anyway and headed for the table, sliding up beside him. "So what are you going to do now?"

He smiled at her, with such charm and innocence that she wanted to hit him. "Now therein lies the problem. I can't go ahead with it and expect you to keep quiet. For one thing, that would make you an accessory, and I don't like to drag innocent people into my business. And as we've already discussed, I can't kill you."

"Why not? It's not that I want you to—I'm just curious as to why you wouldn't."

"I'm a thief, not a killer. I don't even carry a weapon." Before she realized what he was going to do he reached out and brushed a strand of hair away from her face. And his touch made her shiver with longing. "The most logical idea is to take you hostage. That way you're still innocent, you won't interfere with my plans, and I can just let you go at some point."

"And you think you can take me?"

His smile was slow and lascivious. "I think so," he said softly.

He could, too. Not in a battle—if he put his hands on her with any kind of force she'd knock him sideways. She was a strong woman. But then, he was a strong man. And she wasn't quite sure she wanted to fight him.

"Or I can seduce you," he said. "I can make love to you, right here, right now. Push you down on the table and lick every inch of your body. I can make you forget about right and wrong, law and order, middle-class morality and everything you hold dear. I can make you come so much you won't be able to talk or think or stop me from doing anything I want. There's only one problem with that."

"What?" she asked breathlessly. Wanting his hands on her. Wanting him.

"That it would have the same effect on me. I told you, you're my fate. And I've spent most of my life tempting fate. I don't know if I'm ready to give in."

"Let me know when you decide." She slid off the table, turning her back on him. The longer she looked at him the more she wanted him. And she wasn't the type for pirates. "Any idea where my other shoe is? It's going to be a long walk home."

"Probably in the truck," he said, not moving. Still thinking. She was just scrambling up onto the tailgate of the truck when he spoke.

"So I have to give this all up for you?" he asked in a voice that sounded no more than idly curious. "Millions of dollars worth of art treasures that don't really belong to anyone anymore?"

He was mocking her, but she didn't care. "Yes," she said. "All of it."

"I don't even get to keep a reminder? A small Rembrandt? Maybe the Vermeer. As a souvenir?" he asked plaintively.

"You'd get to keep me," she replied, disappearing into the dimly lit cavern of the half-filled truck.

There was no sign of her missing silver sandal. She made one hell of a Cinderella, she thought. Her fairy godmother was a neo-Nazi, her prince charming was a felon, and she wasn't even going to get a happy ending. Though maybe Helms was more like the wicked stepmother, with his goon squad as the ugly stepsisters. It didn't matter. All that mattered was getting out of there, finding her way home where she could throw herself in bed and cry.

She should go to the police. Tell them about Michael Blackheart and the Norenheld Treasure, tell them that Bill Helms had tried to drug and kidnap her. She wouldn't get too far with that part of the story, but at least he'd think twice about coming near her again.

And Michael would either be in jail or he'd make his escape and she'd never see him again. That was the only possible ending in the real world.

The light in the truck was obstructed, and she turned to see Michael standing just a few feet away, a rueful expression on his face. "Yes," he said.

"Yes, what?"

"Yes, I'll give up Rembrandt and Renoir and Vermeer and Lalique and God knows who else for you." He crossed the few steps between them and caught her face in his hands. His beautiful, strong hands. "If you'll let me."

She couldn't answer, because he was kissing her. It didn't matter, because she was kissing him back.

It shouldn't have been glorious. Hasty, fumbling sex on the floor of a rental truck was not the stuff dreams are made of, not Cinderella's happy ending.

But it wasn't hasty. He kissed her, slowly, deliberately, letting her get used to the taste of him, letting her grow bold and demanding in her need to taste him. When his hands slid down over the front of her dress she shivered and moved closer still, and she touched him, sliding her arms around him, letting her hands move up inside the back of the loose T-shirt to feel the heat of his smooth skin.

He pulled the shirt off and tossed it across the darkened truck. And then he reached for her clingy silver dress.

"How does this come off?" he whispered.

Her strangled laugh shocked her. "I don't remember."

"Turn around."

She did, and felt his mouth at the nape of her neck, beneath the heavy fall of her hair. She felt his teeth against her skin, and she moaned, suddenly impatient.

"Rip it," she said.

The tearing sound as the fabric parted beneath his strong hands was one more erotic demand. She tried to turn back but he wouldn't let her. He moved up tight against her, so that she could feel his hot, bare chest against her back, and slowly peeled the torn dress down her body.

She wasn't wearing a bra, but he'd already discovered that in their stolen time at the reception. He pushed the dress down her hips, taking her panties and stockings with it, until it pooled at her ankles, and she was naked, her back pressed up against him in the darkness.

It wasn't fumbling. Michael Blackheart knew exactly what he was doing as his hands touched her breasts, long fingers moving up to cover them. She made a soft, whimpering sound, one of deep-seated longing, as she felt her bones begin to melt.

She tried again to turn in his arms, but he held her tight, and he slid one hand down over her warm flesh, touching her between her legs.

She let out a quiet shriek of protest, momentarily torn out of her erotic daydream. "Michael!" she protested. "What if somebody comes?"

"That's what I had in mind," he murmured against the soft skin of her neck, and he pushed his fingers down against her, hard and clever and merciless.

Well, maybe it was hasty after all. The climax swept over her body with shocking suddenness, and she heard a low, keening sound that could only have come from her own throat.

She was shivering, sobbing when he finally turned her around and pulled her down to the floor of the truck. The fur coat had somehow gotten back there, and she didn't even care as her sensitive skin slid against the soft white fur. All she could think about was him, his hard, sleek flesh, the feel of him as he pushed between her legs, his hands under her hips as he pulled her up against him. This was crazy, irrational, and it didn't matter. All that mattered was Michael, touching her, pushing into her.

She came again when he first filled her. He seemed to know just what to do, how hard to touch her, how soft, when to go fast, when to go achingly, blisteringly slow. He seemed determined to give her the best sex she'd ever had in her life, and she didn't bother to tell him he'd already surpassed that ages ago.

He came when she kissed him. She reached up, breathless, and put her mouth against his, and all his iron control vanished. He pushed into her, fast, hard, and then he went rigid in her arms, filling her, and she followed him one last time, exploding with a heart-stopping joy and endless wonder.

It seemed like hours before she could say anything. She couldn't help it—postcoital guilt was coiling around her like a jealous snake. "You're very good at this," she said in a doubtful whisper, almost hoping he didn't hear her.

But he did. He lifted his head and looked at her with sleepy amusement. "I've had lots of practice."

"I haven't."

His faint smile broadened. "Don't worry about it. I'll give you plenty of chances to learn."

She couldn't decide whether she wanted to pinch him or kiss him, so she contented herself with snuggling closer to him. Quite a feat, considering she was still sandwiched between him and the fur coat, his body wrapped around her, heartbeat to heartbeat.

She sighed, rubbing her face against his shoulder. "This is ridiculous," she murmured breathlessly. "It'll never last."

"You're right," he said in a sleepy voice. "I give us fifty, maybe sixty years, tops."

She smiled in the darkness. "So what do we do next?"

"Find a bed," he said.

Considering that she'd had more orgasms in the last

half hour than she'd had in her entire life that shouldn't have made her react. But it did.

"I mean about the Norenheld Treasure."

"Leave it. We can call Blackheart and tell him where it is once we get to London."

"I thought you said he wasn't in on this?"

"He wasn't. I told you, he might not even know I exist. It was a petty act of revenge and for some reason I don't feel petty anymore." He lifted his head and kissed her lightly. "You're good for me. I have a dismal feeling I'm going to end up completely reformed."

"Dismal," she echoed, kissing him back.

"Utterly," he said, starting to get even more inventive, when suddenly he froze. He swore, almost silently, the obscenity harsh and startling.

"What's wrong?" she whispered.

He pulled out of her arms with fluid grace, and she could barely see him in the shadows. "Someone's here," he said in a barely audible voice. "Stay put while I see who it is." He was already reaching for his discarded clothing.

"But..."

"Do as I say!" All the teasing had left his voice. "Helms and his men play rough, in case you hadn't figured that out yet. Just stay there quietly and I'll see what's going on."

And a moment later he was gone, leaving her alone in the truck, stark naked, with nothing to wear but a torn dress and a slightly abused fur coat.

Chapter Seven

4:00 a.m.

Isabel had never been particularly good at doing what she was told. She picked up her abandoned dress, but Michael had ripped it down to the hem, and it would only work as a scarf, not any kind of cover-up. With a mental apology to all the dead weasels, she pulled the fur coat around her and headed out of the truck.

Her eyes had grown accustomed to the darkness, and she could see they were in some kind of cavernous warehouse. She could see straight up to the ceiling way overhead, through the spider's web of catwalks and pulleys, and the newly risen moon shone down through a huge, dusty skylight.

She kept to the shadows, listening intently, but there was no sound at all. Not from Michael, not from their intruder. The reflection of the moon cast a checkerboard of light in the middle of the floor, and she was about to step forward, into the light, when she was grabbed from behind, silently, efficiently, a hand covering her mouth and silencing her scream.

For the first moment she didn't panic, certain it was Michael. And then a second later she knew it wasn't—the man behind her wasn't the right man, and she began to struggle.

"Hold still and be quiet," a voice hissed in her ear. "Johnson's got a gun."

The voice was vaguely familiar. She stopped struggling, partly because the coat was coming undone and she didn't want her captor to realize she was stark naked underneath, and partly because that oddly familiar voice radiated strength and certainty, not characteristics she associated with Helms's goon squad.

He must have felt her relax, because his grip loosened, and his hand moved from her mouth. Not far, ready to clamp down if she decided to scream, but enough so she could breathe.

She turned her head, and looked into eyes that were eerily like Michael's. It was Patrick Blackheart.

He pulled her back, further into the shadows, and when he spoke his voice was just barely audible. "Where the hell is he?"

"I don't know," she said, pulling the coat tightly around her. From his faintly ironic expression she expected he knew exactly what she was wearing underneath it, but he didn't say anything. "How did you find us?"

"I'm good at my job," he said. "Does he have a gun?"

"Who?"

"My long-lost son."

"No. He says he doesn't like them."

"It figures," Patrick said bitterly. "Goddamned romantic son of a bitch…"

"Hey!" Isabel protested.

"You stay put," Patrick told her, looking particularly ruthless and not at all like the urbane security consultant she'd met in Helms's office. "I'm going to be busy enough trying to save Michael's ass without worrying about you."

"Why didn't you bring the police?"

"I don't think we need to involve the police in this little mess, do you?" he said. "I can take care of my own. When I know they exist."

And a moment later he was gone, disappearing into the shadows without a sound.

She followed him, of course, a few moments later. He'd vanished in the darkness just as effectively as Michael had. And Johnson—how the hell did Blackheart know that Johnson was the one who'd come after them?

Them. It hadn't been her fault that she'd been drugged and dumped into the back of a truck, nor her fault that she'd been carried off with a fortune's worth of old masters. But after that point she'd had a choice, and she'd made it. She'd chosen a jewel thief over a captain of industry, honest larceny over hidden evil. They were bound together, she and Michael, and she didn't regret it for a moment.

Her bare feet were icy on the cement floor, and she tripped against something. She reached down and came up with her abandoned shoe. She held it for a moment, not knowing what to do with it, when something made her look overhead—maybe it was some almost inaudible sound, maybe it was instinct. She peered up and saw Michael edging along a catwalk, barely visible through the shadows, and yet after a few short hours she'd know him anywhere. She watched in fascination, distracted and terrified by his grace and the distance to the ground. She was so intent she almost didn't notice the second figure, coming up behind him, less graceful, less sinuous, just as silent.

It could be Patrick Blackheart, come to pluck his son out of harm's way. But then she saw the gun silhouetted against the moonlight, and she knew it was Johnson.

She opened her mouth to scream, but no sound came out. She was still holding her shoe, and acting on instinct alone, she threw it into a far corner, hoping to distract Henry Johnson from his intended prey.

It worked. Johnson spun around on the catwalk, and the gun spat in the darkness, a burst of muffled noise that was shocking in the stillness. By the time he turned back Michael was gone, and the skylight was open overhead.

Isabel watched in horror as Henry swayed precariously for a moment, and she shut her eyes, half hoping, half afraid he'd fall. But a moment later he'd regained his balance. And he was gone, heading out through the skylight in search of his prey.

THE NIGHT WAS CLEAR and cold, and the bright moonlight cast eerie shadows on the rooftop of the old warehouse. Michael crouched in the corner, half hidden, and waited for his hunter. He'd already recognized his stalker—Johnson, one of Helms's goon squad, the man who'd failed to recognize him earlier. Presumably he'd put the pieces together.

He'd left the skylight open on purpose, to lure Johnson out into the open, away from Isabel. He could only hope that wild shot Johnson had fired down into the darkness hadn't hit her. If it did, he'd pick his beefy body up in his bare hands and throw him through the skylight.

He took a deep, calming breath. He couldn't allow himself to get rattled, to start thinking of unlikely possibilities. Isabel would stay in the truck where it was safe, wouldn't she? Hell, he'd known her for less than twelve hours and he'd already managed to fall in love with her—he also knew her well enough to realize she wouldn't do any such thing.

The main thing was to keep Johnson away from her. He stood a fighting chance against Helms's chief goon—Isabel would be a sitting duck. And it didn't help matters that he'd left her with a shredded dress, no protection at all. Not that he thought Johnson would rape her—Helms's men struck him as basically asexual. They weren't likely to forget their duties. No, they wouldn't rape her, they'd just kill her.

He could see Johnson's white-blond head emerge from the skylight, and for a moment he cursed his refusal to carry a gun. There was nothing he could throw, and he considered making a run for it, slamming the skylight down on his head and sending the bastard hurtling down toward his death, when his hand appeared over the lip of the skylight. Holding a really ugly handgun. So much for heroics, Michael thought, ducking back into the shadows, watching as Johnson clambered out onto the roof. At least Isabel was safe for the time being.

He'd always been good on rooftops and heights, a requirement for a successful cat burglar. Even in his current panicked state he could feel a faint thrill of exhilaration that still lingered after all these years. There were clouds overhead, moving in the direction of the mercilessly bright moonlight, and there were other roofs nearby. If he could just lure Henry away from the building, maybe he'd be able to disable him long enough to get back and get Isabel out of there. The hell with the Norenheld Treasure—someone else could fight that fight. At this point all he wanted was to keep Isabel safe.

He timed it perfectly, but then, he was very good at what he did. The moment the first cloud darkened the rooftop he moved, vaulting over the side onto the flat-topped building adjacent to the warehouse. He heard the muffled whine of the gun, but he'd already reached the other side, ending in a roll that left him crouching up against a huge heating vent. Waiting for Johnson to follow him.

He could see him silhouetted against the sky, peering across the rooftops, and he found he could grin. So his gun-toting pursuer wasn't as happy about high buildings? It wasn't much of an advantage against a Luger, but it was something. Johnson stood there, hesitating, and for a moment Michael was afraid he might turn back, go back down into the old warehouse and drive off with the truck. With Isabel still inside it.

But Isabel wasn't the type to wait patiently inside the truck—she'd be hiding in the warehouse. The question was—how determined would Henry be to find her?

The answer to that question floated eerily between the two buildings. "You left your girlfriend down there," he said. "No protection, no one to watch out for her. Are you sure you want to do that?"

Michael didn't move. If Henry were interested in going after Isabel he wouldn't have announced it. He was just trying to lure Michael into the open. And doing a damned good job of it.

"I might have shot her, you know," Henry continued. "I think I hit something. She wasn't wearing a white fur coat, was she?"

Michael jerked involuntarily, then held still again. Henry would know perfectly well she had the coat— he would have been the one to dump her in the back of the truck with it.

"A shame to ruin such a fine pelt," Henry said, stepping up onto the parapet between the buildings. "I mean the ermine, not Miss Linden's. The bitch didn't know the meaning of the word loyalty." He leaped between the buildings, landing heavily, competently, destroying Michael's hope that he was afraid of heights. "If she's still alive we'll see to her. Von Helmich wants to see her. He has some unfinished business, and I don't think it will be pretty. You might be happier if I had managed to kill her. But then, you'll never know."

He was moving closer, footsteps measured, steady, as he stalked his prey. He passed by Michael's hiding place, totally unaware of him, and once more Michael thanked God that Helms, or Von Helmich, or whoever the hell he was, preferred brawn to brains. There was no doubt that Henry Johnson could blow him to kingdom come. If he had the smarts to find him first.

He waited until the smoothly talking Johnson had reached the far end of the roof, and then he made his move, flying across the uneven surface with the speed of desperation, heading for the next building. It was half a story lower and a deep canal ran between the two buildings, but he had no doubt he could reach it in time. He hadn't counted on the clouds skidding past, unleashing the bright light down around him.

Johnson fired at him, and he dived over the side toward the lower building.

He didn't make it. At the last minute he managed to catch hold of the rusted fire escape ladder, and he hung there, dangling in midair, unable to move, as Johnson came to tower over him.

"Don't even bother," Johnson said calmly. "You try to pull yourself up on that ladder and I'll shoot your hand off. Try to swing your leg around and I'll shoot that, too."

Michael didn't even blink. He could play cat-and-mouse games with the best of them, and he was more than a match for a neo-Nazi bully boy. "So what's the alternative?"

Henry moved to the very edge of the roof, leaning precariously on the parapet. "Well, I could just shoot you through the head. Make it quick and easy. But I never was a man who liked the quick and easy way."

Great, Michael thought. Here he was dangling like

mistletoe off a rusted fire escape, and he had a sadistic psycho playing out his fantasies. To make things even worse, he'd managed to catch hold of the railing with his bad arm, the one Johnson or one of his cronies had already sliced a bullet through. It was stinging like holy hell, fresh blood dripping down his arm from the saturated bandanna, and he wasn't sure how long he could hold on. Long enough for Isabel to make her escape? If she was still walking?

"Then again," Henry mused, climbing up on the crumbling stone barrier to peer down at him, "I might just want to watch until your strength gives out and you fall. Problem is, it's too dark down there to really enjoy it, and then there's the damned canal. You might be lucky enough to land in it and be swept away. They say cats have nine lives, and you may not have gone through all of yours."

Michael glanced down, wondering if he really could target a free fall into the dank water. It seemed unlikely, and besides, there was still the problem of Isabel.

"Or I can enjoy myself," Henry continued. "I could see how many bullets it would take to make you let go. It would be a challenge—to hit you in just the right spot so you still hold on, but you're in incredible pain. Yes, I think I like that idea. It's even more of a challenge that I don't have a clear shot."

"Excuses, excuses," Michael said, flattening himself against the building as best he could. Forcing Johnson to lean further out over the parapet in order to aim the gun at him. Michael could only hope he'd be slightly unsteady on the crumbling stone railing, but he seemed as surefooted as a mountain goat.

"Shall I start with the fingers?" Johnson murmured, half to himself. "Or the foot?" He aimed the gun carefully, leaning a fraction of an inch further into the darkness.

"Get the hell away from my son!"

The voice came out of the night, like the voice of God, and Johnson jerked in surprise, the gun firing wildly into the night. There was a look of complete astonishment on his face as he lost what little remained of his balance, and he fell, past Michael's dangling figure, through the dark chasm, the only sound the bone crunching thuds as he bounced off sections of the old stone building, followed by the soft splash as he ended in the canal. And then all was an eerie silence.

Michael looked up, and a hand was reaching down to him, ready to pull him up. For half a minute he considered letting go, rather than take that offering. But then he reached out and clasped that strong hand, letting his father pull him to safety.

He found himself looking in a pair of eyes that were uncannily like his own. Older, more jaded, but the same deep shade of brown, the same streak of cynicism. He was slighter taller than the Old Man, but built pretty much the same way.

He stood there, saying nothing. Waiting.

"Your arm's bleeding." Patrick Blackheart spoke in a cool, detached voice.

"Just a scrape," Michael said in matching tones.

Patrick stared down into the chasm. "Tide's going

out. With any kind of luck it'll pull Johnson's body with it. I don't think Helms is going to be asking any questions. You might just get away with this.''

''What about the stuff I took?''

''I'll take care of it.''

''Sure you will,'' Michael mocked him. ''I thought you weren't on the job anymore.''

''I'm not. For that matter, neither are you.'' His light tone didn't suggest any room for argument. ''But I'm not going to hand that stuff back to Helms, either. Just leave it up to me. I have resources to bait a little trap for the gentleman. It's the least he deserves, don't you think?''

''And I'm supposed to trust you?''

''Honor among thieves?'' his father said lightly. ''Why didn't you try to find me?''

''I didn't know you existed.''

''That makes two of us.''

''I don't believe you. My grandfather would have come after you. He would have made sure…''

''He would have made sure I was dead. Paulus wasn't the most forgiving old man, and I don't think he had much appreciation for young passion. I assume he's dead?''

''For twelve years now.''

''And your mother?'' There was a softer tone to his voice now, respectful.

''She died when I was three years old. A car accident with the man I always thought was my father.''

''Sorry to ruin your cherished memories,'' Blackheart said lightly. ''How did you find me?''

''Uncle Felix told me.''

"Why am I not surprised that old man is still alive? So you've followed in the family tradition without realizing it."

The thought annoyed him, but there was no way he could dispute it, not on a rooftop with a truckload of stolen art treasures just one building away.

"You'll be following in another tradition," Blackheart added. "Redemption."

"The hell I will…" Michael began, but he was interrupted by more important things. A furry white figure had appeared on the roof of the warehouse, and he could see Isabel looking frantically around her.

And then she saw him. "Michael!" she shrieked, oblivious to everything as she ran barefoot across the roof in his direction.

He was there to catch her when she leaped, and hopefully to shield her from his father's interested gaze as the fur coat flashed open for a moment midair. He pulled her into his arms, holding her in a viselike grip, and he realized he was trembling.

Whether he liked it or not, his father was right. He had to get out of this business. He was too vulnerable.

He was busy kissing her when Patrick Blackheart strolled up beside them. "And that's another thing," he said in his cool, ironic voice. "In my day we kept our minds on business, didn't mix business with pleasure."

"Go away," Michael muttered. "I'm going to marry her."

Isabel jumped, looking up at him in shock. "This is ridiculous," she said with a whispered laugh.

"It is," Michael agreed. "Will you?"

"Yes."

"Spare me," Patrick drawled. "I think I've had about as much as I can take for one night."

"Then go away," Michael repeated patiently.

"How long have you two known each other?"

"Twelve hours," Michael said.

"Forever," Isabel said.

"I don't know if I'm going to be able to stomach this," Blackheart said in an irritable growl. "Come along, children. It's time to go home. Francesca can fix everything."

"Home?" Michael echoed, slightly dazed.

"Home," his father said. "And let me give you a piece of fatherly advice. Next time at least leave your lady something to wear besides a fur coat. She could catch cold."

"Next time?"

"Next time you have sex, which I assume will be fairly often since you're planning on getting married. Not the next time you commit a robbery, which isn't going to happen, since you're coming to work with me and doing your damnedest to keep people from doing just what you've spent your entire life doing. Understood?"

Michael knew he should manage to drum up a little outrage, a little fury at his father's high-handed attitude. He ought to tell Isabel they should go slow, live together for a while, maybe even hightail it for Europe when no one was looking.

He glanced down at his watch, trying to calculate how much time he had to make up his mind. But that venerable timepiece had finally stopped working. And the time was now. There was nothing for him in Europe, not anymore. His life was here, wrapped in his arms and an obscene fur coat, looking up at him out of wary, loving eyes.

"Understood," he said. "Leave us alone now." And he kissed her, ready for the future.

To Krissie,
goddess, idol, friend and one of the good guys

DAY
GAYLE WILSON

ABOUT THE AUTHOR

RITA Award winner for Romantic Suspense and five-time RITA Award finalist Gayle Wilson has written twenty-six novels for Harlequin/Silhouette. A former high school English and world history teacher to gifted students, she writes contemporary romantic suspense and historical fiction set in the English Regency period. She has won numerous awards, including both the 1999 and 1998 Kiss of Death Awards for Outstanding Romantic Suspense, the 1999 Texas Gold Award, the Laurel Wreath Award for Excellence in 1998 and 1999, and the 1999 Dorothy Parker Award for Category Romance, given by Reviewers International Organization.

Gayle still lives in Alabama, where she was born, with her husband of thirty-three years and an ever-growing menagerie of beloved pets. She has one son, who is also a teacher of gifted students. Gayle loves to hear from readers. Write to her at P.O. Box 3277, Hueytown, AL 35023.

Books by Gayle Wilson

HARLEQUIN INTRIGUE

Chapter One

"Duncan?"

The call had come in on his cell phone, insuring that the voice he heard would be a friend's, not a client's. This particular voice was, however, the last he would have expected from that exclusive circle Duncan Culhane considered friends. Fewer than a dozen people had been given this number, and the woman who had just said his name wasn't one of them.

Not that he wouldn't have given it to her. Just as he would have given her anything else she might have asked him for. Only she hadn't asked. Never. Not for anything.

And although it had been at least five years since he'd heard her voice, nothing had changed about its effect. Even now, even after all this time, his groin tightened, filled with a heated rush of blood.

The result of a desire he'd never confessed to a living soul. Especially not to her.

"Andrea?"

He was pleased with the steadiness of that. Especially pleased to have managed that slightly questioning intonation, as if he were unsure of his identification. He wasn't. He would have recognized her voice if he were put into a dark room with a thousand women.

Andrea Sorrenson wouldn't even have to speak for him to know her. He'd be able to pick her out in that darkness by doing what he had done every time he'd been around her. He would breathe in the air that surrounded her, filled with the subtle fragrance of her skin, while he kissed her cheek or her hand.

There had never been any other physical contact between them. She had been his best friend's wife, so he had no option other than to keep his distance. And that was probably more necessary now than it had been when Paul Sorrenson was alive.

"Griff suggested I call you," she said. "I hope that's all right. He said you were out here."

I should have known, Duncan thought, easing down into the leather chair behind the desk where he was working. Andrea would never have called him on her own. He should have realized that before he'd allowed himself to feel this surge of excitement.

"Of course it's all right. It's wonderful to hear from you. It's been a long time."

There was a small, awkward silence, as if she were trying to think of something to say in response. Instead, she took a breath, deep enough that the inhalation was audible.

"I have…a problem, Duncan."

Which was why she had contacted Griff, of course. Anyone seeking the services of The Phoenix Brotherhood would normally have gone through an intermediary, a screening process of sorts. Because Paul Sorrenson had been a member of the clandestine and highly elite antiterrorist group Griff Cabot had put together for the CIA, Andrea would have had immediate access to them.

The members of Phoenix were, like Duncan himself, all former operatives who had gone to work for Cabot's private organization after the CIA dissolved the External Security Team. The agency had decided, foolishly it turned out, that the post-Cold War world no longer had any use for their services.

Even as their government professed to no longer need the specialized skills the team possessed, there seemed to be a multitude of others who found them valuable. Enormously valuable, judging by the midyear dividend they had shared.

"What kind of problem?" he asked, still working on tamping down the emotional response her voice evoked.

He switched the phone to his right hand, the one that was state of the art, plastic and electronics, decently covered with the "realistic" synthetic skin its creators were so proud of. As soon as he had, he used the other to select a pen from the holder on the desk.

He had never quite mastered the art of writing with his nondominant hand, at least not to his own satisfaction. If the writing hadn't grown cold, however, he could usually manage to decipher any notes he jotted about the cases he was assigned. *Usually*.

"It's my grandparents," Andrea said.

The pen lifted, hesitating over the pad as Duncan digested the information. Given that Andrea was in her mid-thirties, a few years younger than he, her grandparents would be at least in their seventies.

"They're in some kind of trouble?"

"Not trouble, really. It's a little complicated.

Maybe not anything you'd feel comfortable getting involved with. Griff said that since you were in San Francisco…'' She hesitated again, and this time he waited through the pause. "I thought we could meet somewhere and talk.''

The suggestion lay between them for several long seconds, sending that same flood of heat coursing through his body. It was joined this time by a touch of anxiety, maybe even of dread. Something Duncan Culhane had believed he'd put behind him a long time ago.

Perhaps that was why he found himself agreeing. That and the fact that if it hadn't been for him, Paul Sorrenson would be around to handle this. Since he wasn't…

"Of course,'' Duncan said, feeling his dread increase, even as he said the words. "Name the time and place.''

As SOON AS SHE'D SUGGESTED the restaurant, Andrea had begun to have second thoughts. Maybe by opting for lunch, she had turned what was supposed to be strictly a business meeting into something else.

You're overanalyzing, she chided herself.

Duncan was an old friend. She'd been referred to him by his boss. Whatever interpretation anyone else might put on this invitation, Duncan would know exactly what it was.

She took a deep breath, something she'd been doing rather frequently since she'd dialed his number, and realized that her hands were trembling. And he might also know exactly what that was.

Except he hadn't, she reassured herself. Duncan had never realized how she'd felt about him. And she couldn't credit that failure to her ability to dissemble or to any degree of sophistication. When she'd fallen in love with Duncan Culhane, more than ten years ago, she hadn't had much of either.

She had been sure he'd see right through her. Maybe secretly anticipating the moment when he did.

He had never seemed to notice her infatuation. After all, she wasn't the kind of woman Duncan had ever been attracted to. He had probably not given her a second thought as a possible romantic interest.

Following on the heels of that unconscious rejection, Paul's attention had been a much-needed balm for her battered ego. So much so that she had occasionally wondered if that was the reason she'd finally agreed to marry him. And then she would feel disloyal for even considering the possibility.

"Andrea?"

She looked up from the water glass she'd been toying with and straight into the most vivid blue eyes she'd ever seen. When she'd first met Duncan Culhane, she had thought how unfair it was that they should be wasted on a man.

It was equally unfair that they hadn't changed. The passage of years hadn't faded their blue, as it so often did. They were exactly the same as the last time she'd seen him.

And then, when she'd had time to take in the rest of his features, she realized there were differences there. None that made him less attractive, not to her, but the years that had passed had definitely etched changes on that ruggedly handsome face.

It was leaner, the small lines that radiated from the outer corners of those remarkable eyes more deeply graven. Even the well-shaped lips seemed harder.

Thinner, somehow. And there was a touch of gray at
his temples, more noticeable because of the raven's
wing gloss of the rest.

"How are you?" she said, putting out her hand.

Still nervous about this meeting, she had made the
familiar gesture without thinking. Now that she had,
she wasn't sure which would be worse: to snatch her
hand back guiltily or to pretend she hadn't known.

The delay in his response was less obvious than the
one in their phone conversation. During that, she had
had time to come to the unwelcome conclusion that,
despite what Griff had told her, Duncan was going to
refuse to meet her.

This hesitation was brief enough that she only had
time for a scintilla of guilt and embarrassment before
the warm, hard fingers of his left hand, definitely flesh
and bone, closed around hers. He brought her hand
to his mouth, breathing a near-kiss on the back before
he straightened, releasing it.

"I think we're too well acquainted to settle for a
handshake," he said easily. "How are *you?*"

"I'm fine," she lied, wishing she'd had the presence of mind to order a glass of wine before he arrived. She had never dreamed this would be so hard.

"I can tell," he said, smiling at her as he pulled
out the chair on the opposite side of the table, skillfully using the hand he had just avoided offering to
her.

She kept her eyes locked on his face, concentrating
on holding on to her smile without letting it get stiff.
Dear God, she thought, *this is Duncan. Why the hell
is this so hard?* And then answered her own question.
Because it's Duncan, of course.

"If that's supposed to be flattery," she said, still smiling, "I'm not impressed. You used to be better at that."

She had spent a couple of hours deciding what to wear. Another making sure her hair and makeup were perfect. And the best he could do...

"You don't need flattery," he said. "Not if you have a mirror. People are supposed to have changed in five years."

"I was thinking the same thing."

He didn't laugh. Nor did he do any of the self-effacing things any other man she knew might have done. He held her eyes instead, seemingly without embarrassment.

She couldn't say the same. She could feel the heat rising into her throat and spreading upward. Because of her fair skin, there was no doubt he would be aware of that telltale blush.

"Still involved in art?" he asked easily, ignoring her discomfort.

"Graphic design," she affirmed, grasping the life-line he'd tossed her. "I have my own firm now. I'm an employer, if you can believe that," she said, smiling at him.

"I never had any doubt you'd be a success at anything you undertook."

"I wish you'd been around to tell me that when I finally decided to launch out on my own. I could have used a boost of confidence."

He smiled, but didn't pursue the subject of her lack of self-confidence. She was probably boring him silly, she realized.

"Do you want to talk about your 'problem' before

or after we eat?'' he asked, reinforcing that impression.

''Probably both,'' she said. ''I told you. It's…a little complicated.''

Actually it wasn't. She could have explained all of it on the phone. But even when she *had* explained, she doubted he'd question what she had just said. He would simply listen with the same careful attention he had always devoted to any subject he cared about.

''Something about your grandparents you said.''

He accepted the menu the waiter offered, his eyes leaving her face for the first time since he'd sat down. Released from their intensity, she allowed her own gaze to fall to the menu as well, grateful for the chance to regroup.

She waited until the waiter had taken their orders and left before she attempted to answer his question. And when she began, choosing her words carefully, she could only hope Griff Cabot had known what he was talking about.

''THEY WERE SMUGGLED OUT of Hungary by a Catholic organization, which had somehow realized what was happening. Or rather, what was about to happen. Grandfather didn't want to go, but my grandmother was carrying their first child. She was terrified by the rumors that were beginning to seep through Eastern Europe. I'm not sure she really believed them—I'm not sure anyone did—but she didn't feel they could take a chance.''

''They were lucky,'' he said.

Given what she had told him, Duncan had already begun imagining the kinds of scenarios that might have prompted Andrea to call Phoenix on her grandparents' behalf. Based on the fact that they had been successful in their escape, he had discarded the possibility that they had seen some concentration camp guard or war criminal they wanted brought to justice.

The most likely prospect, then, involved the recovery of monies that had been left in some account. In Switzerland perhaps. The international banking community had been concerned for some time with the restitution of Jewish fortunes that had been "absorbed" by the various financial institutions to which they had been entrusted.

"They fled with nothing but the clothes on their backs," Andrea went on. "They *were* lucky to be alive, and too soon they understood how lucky. At the same time they lost everything. Every family memento. Every photograph. Every letter. Eventually they learned that in that Holocaust that swept across Europe, they had also lost every relative either of them had ever known."

"I'm so sorry," he said softly.

She shook her head, lifting her hands in a small gesture of acceptance or resignation, perhaps. "Their story isn't unusual. I know that. So do they. Perhaps the only unusual part was the welcome my grandfather found here after the war. He was a doctor. He had been trained in some of the finest universities in Europe. He was only a quarter Jewish, so before the Nazi occupation, he was allowed to practice and even to teach at the University of Budapest. Eventually, however..."

Duncan again waited through the pause, willing to be patient and let her tell this her way. Besides, it gave him a chance to study her more openly than he had allowed himself to do up to this point. And despite what he'd said before he sat down, there *had* been changes.

The wildly curling dark hair, which had been worn long and loose when he'd first met her, had been tamed. Although the arrangement looked artless, layered softly around her face, he suspected that casualness had been achieved by a very professional, and probably expensive, stylist.

And there was at least one other noticeable change. The slight wariness in the clear hazel eyes hadn't been there the last time he'd seen Andrea Sorrenson. Of course, that had been *before* her husband's death.

Duncan hadn't been in any condition to attend Paul's funeral. He had still been in the hospital, which had probably been a blessing. At least it had offered him an excuse not to have to face her.

"And then, two weeks ago, they saw this," she said, bringing his attention back to the present, as her story had now returned to it.

She was holding out a glossy brochure, her arm stretched across the table. He reached for it with his right hand, a habit he had never been able to break. He hadn't even realized what he'd done until they'd made the exchange.

For a second or two, however, their fingers were on the paper at the same time. Hers, long and slender. Just as they had always been, the nails closely trimmed and unpolished. And his...

He didn't look at her face. Thankfully the brochure gave him a valid reason not to raise his eyes. As he scanned it, he realized it was a presale advertisement from a well-known San Francisco auction house, noted for handling items that were likely to bring bids in the hundreds of thousands or even more.

Holding the minicatalog carefully in his right hand, he opened it with his left, congratulating himself on not dropping the damn thing into the flower arrangement. Inside were rows of pictures. Obviously items that were to be offered at the sale. One had been circled in red.

Although the pictures were very small, the object appeared to be a crystal box, and the name below it was one he recognized. He looked up, allowing the front of the brochure to fall closed over the thumb of the prosthesis. He raised his brows in inquiry, although he thought he now knew where this was going.

"It was my grandmother's. It's a music box, and as far as I can ascertain, the only one René Lalique ever made. Her father ordered it from the Paris workshop as her wedding present."

This, too, was a story old enough and familiar enough not to require discussion. As the Nazi juggernaut rolled across Europe, it had swallowed innumerable artifacts and objets d'art, many of which had never resurfaced. Most of them, in the intervening half century, had found their way into private collections, either here or on the continent.

"Grandmother recognized it immediately, but proving she's the rightful owner is impossible. I tried, hoping the special order would still be on file with the Paris branch."

"And it wasn't," Duncan said. It was hardly surprising, of course, given the turmoil of the period, that records had disappeared, even at such a prestigious establishment.

"Perhaps there never was a written record. Maybe Lalique made it as a personal favor for my great-grandfather, and a verbal agreement was all they ever had. Grandmother says he made other things for the family. This one, however, was very special, certainly to her. Not only a wedding present, but one chosen by her father.''

''You want me to approach the auction house and present a claim,'' he said. It wasn't even framed as a question.

Again Duncan wondered why Griff had suggested him for this. Art was hardly his area of expertise. Granted, he was already on the West Coast, but considering the frequency of flights from New York, Griff himself could have been in San Francisco within a few hours. And Cabot's silver-spoon background would certainly make him more qualified to handle this kind of negotiation than Duncan was.

Andrea had hesitated a moment before she said, ''I've already approached them. After acquiring his permission, they put me in touch with the owner of the collection.''

''The owner?'' he asked, his eyes falling again to the front of the brochure to see if the name were listed. It was. As he found it, Andrea pronounced it for him.

''Bill Helms.''

One of that handful of computer geniuses whose names were as familiar to Americans as the president's, Helms had originally made his money designing computer operating systems. Through the years he had made a lot more of it.

''He was surprisingly gracious,'' she went on. ''When I explained to him why I was calling, he agreed to return the music box as soon as the preview was over. And without any documentation to support my grandmother's claim. Considering its value as a one-of-a-kind design, that was incredibly generous. He seemed genuinely appalled that an item with such a…questionable history had made its way into his uncle's collection.''

''No questions asked,'' Duncan suggested.

Which might mean that the acquisition of those articles, and perhaps of others within that collection, wouldn't stand up to public scrutiny. The owner was willing to take the loss represented by the return of the music box in order to prevent questions from being asked.

''*I* didn't ask any. My grandmother is eighty-two. Grandfather is five years older and suffering from prostate cancer. I was enormously grateful for his agreement, no matter the terms.''

Obviously Duncan hadn't been called in to pass judgment on those negotiations or on any of the principals involved, the collector included.

''You want me to provide security for the exchange,'' he guessed.

A large part of what The Phoenix Brotherhood did involved protective services of one kind or another. Griff had never before asked him to protect a work of art, but Duncan didn't imagine the procedures for doing so were very different from any of the other exchanges he'd overseen. At least this merchandise wasn't alive. If he screwed up, nobody died.

''I did warn you,'' Andrea said. ''This is the part where it gets complicated.''

She lifted her water glass and brought it to her lips. She took a long swallow, and then she looked at him over the rim, without putting the glass back on the table.

"Someone stole it," she said.

"Stole it?" he repeated blankly. And then it hit him. "Someone stole the music box?"

She nodded. "Along with all the other items from the collection, many of them far more valuable than grandmother's. When I went to the auction house this morning to make the final arrangements, the place was in a very discreet uproar. I was told about the theft in strict confidence. It hasn't been made public yet. Too many reputations to consider, I suppose. Although, with the sale scheduled for tonight, I don't see how they can suppress the news much longer."

"This happened last night?"

Again she nodded, her eyes clouding a little, focusing on some memory instead of on his face.

"There was a reception at the Carlyle Hotel. To give people a chance to preview the collection. The guest list was, as you can imagine, very select. Most of the names you'd recognize."

"Security?"

Her eyes came up to his, widened a little in surprise at the abruptness of his tone.

"What kind of security did they have?" he clarified.

At last he had made some sense of Griff's decision. Duncan was the team's expert in terms of designing security. When he saw whatever setup they had used to protect the collection, he would probably be able to figure out what had gone wrong. And if he understood how the thief had pulled this off, he might have some clue as to who was involved.

Even the best thief couldn't avoid leaving a certain professional "signature." He might have a favorite means of entrance or a particular method for avoiding the detection devices. Those were all things Interpol and major law enforcement agencies kept track of because they hinted at the identity of those involved in a theft. He could only hope that was the case here.

"I didn't question the arrangements," Andrea said. "Mr. Helms told me a top-of-the-line firm was handling security, with the best antitheft and surveillance equipment available. And of course he can afford the best. Still…it's gone."

Duncan tried to decide who might have been called in to handle the security for a project like this. Of course, there was no reason that couldn't have been handled "in house." Helms would undoubtedly have people with the expertise to cover it on his payroll.

Andrea had implied, however, that he'd hired someone from outside to handle the preview. To cover his tracks because the theft wasn't really a theft, but some kind of insurance fraud?

"He wants his collection back, of course," Andrea said. "And if he doesn't get it—"

"Your grandmother doesn't get her music box."

"He's offering a substantial reward."

"No questions asked," Duncan said again.

Apparently this time the edge of sarcasm came through, because Andrea said, "You keep saying that."

"It sounds as if he can't afford to have questions asked about the origins of this collection. I'm surprised he allowed those pictures to be made public."

She looked puzzled. "It was his uncle's collection. He had nothing to do with acquiring it. As far as the catalog is concerned, it was a fairly select mailing. My grandparents weren't included. Grandmother saw the brochure at a friend's. She recognized the music box immediately.

"Her first thought was to try to buy it back. Although my grandfather made a very good living, they've given most of it away to the various causes they've supported through the years. If they had been able to scrape together what the box would bring at auction, it would have wiped out their savings. Besides—"

"It's theirs," Duncan said simply.

"It was," she agreed. "I want it to be again. Griff said you're the best for something like this. I'm not sure what you charge. He wouldn't talk money to me, but maybe combined with the reward Helms is offering—"

"I won't talk money with you either. Not for something like this. You have to know me better than that."

Just as Griff, Jordan Cross and Hawk had envisioned, Phoenix had proved profitable enough to support all of them. And profitable to allow them to undertake cases for those who couldn't afford their fee. Those they decided on together, one vote per man. And thus far, each of those decisions had been unanimous.

This was obviously not one of those pro bono deals, since no vote had been called, but Duncan couldn't imagine any member of The Phoenix Brotherhood charging Andrea, no matter what she needed. That was apparently what Cabot had decided as well since he'd given her Duncan's private number.

"I know how you felt about Paul," she said. "And I know that you feel somehow…responsible for what happened to him. Which is patently ridiculous, Duncan. Paul was a big boy. He knew what he was getting into.''

''He was my partner.''

''And your friend. But that didn't make you responsible for his life. And it doesn't make you responsible for me. Or for my grandparents. I want you to do this, not because I was Paul's wife, but because you're the best person for the job. And because you have some expectation of being suitably rewarded—''

''Have you told Helms about me?'' he interrupted.

He didn't care about the money. Whatever he felt about Paul's death, he would have done this, no matter what. *And anything else she asked.*

He had thought that when he'd heard her voice this morning. It was no less true now.

''He's arranging a meeting for you with his security consultant in…'' She glanced at her watch, before she looked up to smile at him. ''Forty-five minutes. We'll have to eat and run, I'm afraid.''

It wouldn't be the first time he'd been forced to do that, Duncan thought. At least this time no one would be shooting at him.

Chapter Two

"This is Patrick Blackheart, Mrs. Sorrenson. My *so-called* security consultant," Helms said, his displeasure with Blackheart's failure to protect his collection obvious. "Mrs. Sorrenson's grandmother owned one of the items that was stolen last night."

"An item which would have come back into her possession only through Mr. Helms's generosity," Andrea said. She smiled, offering her hand to Blackheart.

"Mrs. Sorrenson," Patrick Blackheart said. He held her hand briefly, returning her smile. "Please give my condolences to your grandmother. I assure you that having *anything* stolen last night was not part of *my* plan."

Duncan noticed the small emphasis on the pronoun, filing it away for further consideration as Helms plowed on with the introductions.

"And this is Duncan Culhane, Mrs. Sorrenson's friend, who is a security expert. I've asked him to take a look at your arrangements to see if he can figure out what you did wrong."

There was probably nothing Helms could have said

that would raise Blackheart's hackles more than that, Duncan thought. And it would only make his own job harder.

What he'd agreed to do was already tough enough, he had decided. Since this appointment at the hotel where the reception had been held last night had been set up before he'd met Andrea, Duncan hadn't had time to research either of the men he was meeting. He was at least familiar with Helms's biography, as was most of America.

In person, Bill Helms had seemed less imposing than when all Duncan knew about him was his supposed IQ and the size of his fortune. And he knew nothing about Blackheart, other than what Helms had told Andrea before the robbery.

His first impressions of the security consultant were mixed. Rather than reacting with anger to Helms's comments, the brown eyes had remained cool, almost amused. They met Duncan's with a steadiness that bespoke a man who was very sure of himself. Comfortable in his own skin.

Probably in his early fifties, Blackheart was slender and looked extremely fit. He also appeared to be perfectly relaxed, despite what had happened last night. In spite of the seeming sincerity of his condolences to Andrea's grandmother, he didn't appear to be suffering much remorse over the loss of several million dollars worth of items from his employer's collection.

That might mean he believed he'd done everything he could to prevent such a loss and therefore felt no guilt. Or it might mean something else entirely. It was far too early for Duncan to attempt to make that assessment, although there was something about the amusement in Blackheart's eyes that argued for the latter.

Another jarring note was the man's almost theatrical attire. He was wearing a black turtleneck and black jeans. Like some damn cat burglar, Duncan thought, hiding his own amusement. Of course, with a name like Blackheart...

Duncan didn't offer his hand, an impulse he *had* learned to control. Nor did the consultant. He nodded instead, the gesture accompanied by a slight movement at the corner of his mouth.

It was subtle enough that Duncan would have missed it if he hadn't been watching Blackheart's face. He had learned through the years that the non-verbal ways in which people reacted when they discovered *why* Duncan didn't offer to shake hands was as revealing as what they said or did.

"Although Mr. Helms had dismissed my services *before* the actual theft," Blackheart said, "last night's security plan was mine. And what went wrong with it is really very simple. Somehow the thieves discovered that the armored trucks that were supposed to carry the treasure to the auction house were decoys. The art had been loaded into the caterer's truck, just as I'd intended from the beginning. Then Mr. Helms's staff allowed someone to drive it off into the night."

"*Your* plan and therefore *your* responsibility," Helms said, a flush of anger under that freckled, milk-white skin. "What I want to know is *how* they learned about the deception."

Blackheart's shoulders lifted in a small shrug. "No matter how clever we think we are, there is always a smarter, more cunning thief on the horizon, ready to outwit us. Sometimes we win, and sometimes, as we did last night, we lose.''

Except you aren't the kind who likes to lose, Duncan thought.

Even if Blackheart had been dismissed before the theft, he readily admitted that the plan to safeguard the collection was his. Duncan wondered why he was trying so hard to pretend this didn't bother him. After all, there would certainly be financial repercussions to his firm from this theft, if only in a loss of reputation.

"Any idea how they learned about the switch?" he asked aloud.

The cool brown eyes held on his a fraction of a second before Blackheart responded. "None at all. During the preview, we were using electromagnetic field protection because Mr. Helms didn't want his guests' view of the objects to be obstructed. There was also a closed circuit TV system set up, with cameras in every corner of the reception room."

He reeled off the security measures by rote. Since Helms had hired him, Blackheart would be more than competent, of course. Duncan couldn't find fault with those arrangements, not if the equipment had been properly placed and activated.

"We always knew the collection would be most vulnerable during the process of transporting it from the Carlyle to the auction house. We decided to foil any attempt to steal it then by putting the art in the catering boxes and the catering supplies in the wooden crates. All of that was done inside the hotel, with the security measures I mentioned in place. Nothing went wrong during the process."

"You've watched the tapes?"

"All of them. There's nothing happening except what was *supposed* to happen."

"Then…?"

"The crates, full of the caterer's supplies, were loaded into the armored trucks under heavy security. The cardboard boxes containing the collection were handled by the kitchen staff and loaded onto the catering truck. As soon as that was finished, someone unknown drove off with it."

"Who was watching that loading?"

"Mr. Helms's staff stepped in at the last minute to…supervise."

There was nothing Duncan could read in Blackheart's voice. Not anger or even bitterness over his replacement. Eventually Duncan would have to know what had prompted that, but he let it go for the moment.

"No electronic surveillance set up?"

There was the smallest hesitation before Blackheart said, "There was a van positioned in the alley."

"Closed-circuit."

"Of course."

"And they didn't see anything?"

"There was…interference. Quite a bit of it actually. At least during the crucial minutes."

"Any explanation for that."

"None at all," Blackheart said readily, that same hint of mockery in his eyes, although his voice was matter-of-fact.

"And you've looked at that tape as well."

"There's nothing on it," Blackheart said simply.

"Had the items that were stolen been fitted with identidots?"

A trade word for putting microchips on or in works of art. Most of the major museums did it as a matter of course. Then, if something was stolen, the object could be easily identified if it were ever offered for sale, providing that sale was to a reputable dealer or to another museum. Most of them weren't, of course. Stolen art usually went directly into private collections, no questions asked.

"Mr. Helms had indicated that he preferred they not be marked," Blackheart said, his voice still neutral.

No questions asked. The phrase reverberated in Duncan's head because that lack of precaution on Helms's part made no sense. No more than someone knowing Blackheart's plan or the unexplained failure of state-of-the-art security equipment during the crucial moments of the robbery.

"I didn't want to present difficulties or additional expense for the purchasers in having to have them removed," Helms explained, as if what he had just said should make perfect sense.

"But the collection was insured?" Duncan asked.

"Of course, but the company isn't happy. They want a full investigation before they'll pay. We had to guarantee them a certain standard of security before they would agree to the preview. I assured them that Blackheart, Inc. was providing it. Mr. Blackheart failed to fulfill his part of the contract. I'm sure they'll be interested in discussing that failure with *you*," Helms said to Blackheart, his voice cold.

For the first time Duncan glimpsed the ruthlessness that would have been necessary to carry this slight, bespectacled man to the heights of success he had

achieved. And hearing that tone, he was glad it would
be Blackheart, rather than he, who would be on the
receiving end of all the questions this theft would
generate.

Helms's security consultant was correct, however,
in what he'd said earlier. There were bound to be
losses. No matter how sophisticated the antitheft systems became, there was always someone clever
enough or daring enough to try to outsmart them.
Sometimes, despite everything, they succeeded.

Judging by his almost arrogant air of assurance,
Duncan believed it had been a long time since Patrick
Blackheart had been outsmarted. And he couldn't figure out why the man wasn't more disturbed by the
fact that he obviously had been last night.

That would definitely be a question for Griff. Using
his contacts within the CIA, Cabot had the resources
to find out everything there was to know about these
two. The good *and* the bad.

"Do you think you can help us, Mr. Culhane?"
Helms asked, bringing Duncan's gaze back to his
face. "I assure you Blackheart will cooperate completely."

Despite the fact that he was in the act of pushing
his glasses up onto his nose as he said it, he had
managed to make that sound like a threat. Before he
answered, Duncan glanced back at Helms's security
consultant. Blackheart's eyes were on his face rather
than on his employer's.

Duncan waited a second or two, giving Blackheart
a chance to respond to what had clearly been a challenge. When he didn't, Duncan turned again to
Helms.

"I work for Mrs. Sorrenson," he said. Since Helms had used the plural pronoun in his request, the reminder seemed appropriate. "However, since it's obvious the items were all taken by the same thief, when I find hers…"

"You will also recover Mr. Helms's," Blackheart finished for him. "I'm sure he'll be grateful. I imagine we'll all be grateful to put this behind us."

There had not been a hint of gratitude in the comment. Nor would Duncan expect that. After all, if he were successful in recovering the stolen items, it would put Blackheart's firm in an even less favorable light with Helms.

"I'd like to take a look at the van," Duncan said.

"You want to examine the equipment to see if you can explain its unexpected failure," Patrick Blackheart suggested.

"If you don't have any objections."

"It doesn't matter if he does," Helms said. "You're free to examine whatever you want. I'm still paying the bills here."

"I'll wait for you in the foyer, Duncan," Andrea said. "I need to call Grandmother and tell her why I haven't arrived with her music box."

Duncan nodded. He turned to Blackheart, one brow lifted. The security consultant inclined his head, that subtle, almost unnoticeable movement flickering again at the corner of his mouth. He extended his arm, indicating the way to the service door that would lead to the alley behind the hotel. The gesture was almost grandiose, as subtly mocking as his eyes had been.

"Be my guest, Mr. Culhane," Blackheart said.

"I've always enjoyed the occasional professional collaboration."

"WHAT DID YOU THINK?" Andrea asked, as soon as the massive doors of the hotel closed behind them.

"I think I wouldn't want to be in Blackheart's shoes," Duncan said truthfully. "I doubt Helms will be that restrained once we're gone."

"I meant about the equipment."

"Exactly what he said. State of the art."

"Then what went wrong?" Andrea asked. "Despite all that business about smarter thieves."

"The system was disabled."

"How?"

"I don't know."

He mentally reviewed his impressions of the man who had shown off his equipment with an openness that argued against his having anything to hide.

"It had to be someone on the inside," Duncan said.

"Blackheart?"

"Or someone working for him. Someone he trusted."

"He didn't mention anyone else."

"A company with a reputation good enough to convince Helms to hire them isn't a one-man show."

"So, what now? Are you going to tell the police that? Or Helms?"

"Before we do anything else, we're going to call in the reinforcements."

"Reinforcements?"

"There's no reason not to use the advantages Griff's contacts at the agency offer." After all, he thought, Griff had gotten him into this.

Andrea nodded. ''You can call him from the house. We're only a few blocks away. That will be quicker than going back to your hotel.''

Which was all the way across town. Since he wanted to get Griff onto this as soon as possible, going to Andrea's made eminent sense. Except Duncan wasn't looking forward to seeing where Andrea had lived with Paul. Actually, he wasn't looking forward to being alone with her. Other than during the cab ride from the restaurant to the hotel, there had been people around them all afternoon.

''Is that okay?'' she questioned hesitantly. ''Or do you need to get back to whatever you were doing when I called you this morning?''

''I need to touch base with them,'' he said.

That would be politic, but not urgent. After all, the job was finished. He had only been tying up loose ends before he was scheduled to return to New York.

Since he wasn't leaving, he supposed he should call the hotel and tell them he would be staying a few more days. And notify the airline that he'd be taking a later flight.

''So…my place?'' Andrea asked again, looking at him over her shoulder as she moved to the curb to flag a cab.

And because he couldn't think of a single legitimate excuse to refuse, Duncan nodded.

''BLACKHEART, INC. John Patrick Blackheart,'' Duncan read from the business card he'd requested before he'd left the hotel.

''Sounds like an alias if I've ever heard one,'' Griff said, amusement coloring his deep voice.

"He dresses the part," Duncan said.

"You think he was in on it?"

Unconsciously Duncan's lips pursed as he reexamined his impressions. Blackheart's openness in revealing his failures argued against that. Of course, that might just as easily be put down to arrogance. A catch-me-if-you-can sort of taunting, which seemed in character.

"I don't see how they could have carried it off without the complicity of *someone* on the inside. That's something else I want you to check. Find out who works with Blackheart."

"You didn't answer my question," Griff said patiently.

He should have known Griff would notice. However, he didn't have an answer yet. Not to that. Not to anything.

"I don't know. There is *something* there." There had been. Something Blackheart knew that he hadn't shared. It had lurked just behind the mockery in his eyes. "Give me a couple of days. *And* everything you can find out about the man. Maybe then I can tell you if he was involved."

"So, how's Andrea?" Griff asked.

There were a dozen possible connotations to the question. Duncan chose the easiest to answer.

"Disappointed, of course. Her grandmother had been expecting to get her property back this afternoon. It's bad enough to see a personal item put on the auction block, but then to have been promised its return, only to discover that someone else has stolen it before you can get it back..."

"Someone else?"

"Someone besides whoever took it during the war."

"The usual suspects, I assume," Griff said.

"Probably. It might be interesting to try to trace the origins of the other items in Helms's collection. He told Andrea that his uncle had amassed it. Norwegian. The uncle, I mean. There was more than one Quisling in Norway."

"You suspect more of it might be Nazi loot?"

"Even if it is, that doesn't prove either Helms or his uncle was aware of that."

"But it's possible."

"At this point anything is possible. I need your help to narrow those possibilities. I asked Helms to give me a list of the items that were stolen last night, along with a description of each. I'll fax that to you when I get back to the hotel. Maybe the thief was recovering somebody else's 'lost' property. If Helms hadn't agreed to give back Andrea's grandmother's music box, I might have been tempted to try something like that myself."

There were a few beats of silence on the other end of the line. During them, Duncan realized Griff was at a loss as to how to answer what had essentially been an idle comment. Because Cabot didn't think Duncan could carry that off? At least not now?

"I'll get back to you as soon as I have something," Griff said instead of responding. "Are you staying at the same hotel?"

"For tonight. I may try to find something closer if this doesn't resolve fairly quickly."

"I'll do my best," Griff promised.

It seemed to Duncan as he hung up that he should

have been the one making that promise. Until a few background questions had been answered, however—

"What did Griff think?" Andrea asked.

He turned and found her standing in the doorway, watching him. He had no idea how long she had been there. While he'd been on the phone, she'd changed out of her suit and into a long, bronze-colored sweater worn over a pair of aged, narrow-legged jeans. The years fell away, reminding him of the first time he'd seen her. And that was not necessarily a good thing, he acknowledged.

Andy had been only a few years out of art school, spending the summer working as a docent in one of the museums in the capital. She had somehow been invited to a party a few of Griff's people had also attended.

He had thought that night that she was one of the most genuinely alive people he'd ever met, interested in everything her experience in Washington had to offer. And very much against his better judgment, he'd arranged to run into her on more than a few occasions, eventually introducing her to his friend Paul. And after that—

He buried the memory, forcing himself to concentrate on the here and now. "He's going to do some background checks on Blackheart, his employees and on Helms. We should know something by tomorrow."

"On *Helms?*"

"He wouldn't be the first person to steal from himself in order to collect on the insurance."

"As rich as he is? Wouldn't that be taking a huge, unnecessary risk?"

"*If* he's as rich as he's supposed to be. And if he is, he didn't get there by being afraid to take risks. The challenge might appeal to him."

Andrea shook her head, smiling a little. "I know you're right, but somehow after meeting him…"

"He's wealthy enough that if he didn't have a use for that persona, it would be easy enough to abandon it. I think he doesn't *because* it enables him to take people off guard."

She nodded, considering that. "And Blackheart? That kind of challenge might appeal to him as well. I think he'd probably relish getting away with stealing something he's supposed to be guarding."

There was a hint of admiration in her voice. Of course, a lot of women were drawn to the rogues of the world. The enigmatic Blackheart would certainly qualify.

Even as he thought it, Duncan wondered on what basis he'd assigned the characterization to Blackheart. He knew nothing about the man, other than the fact that Helms had hired him. And that he had seemed to know what he was talking about.

"I think they're both the kind who like living on the edge," he said evasively.

"You wouldn't know anything about that, of course," Andrea said, her smile teasing.

Duncan had lived on the edge so long that, despite the horror of Paul's death, and even with his own injuries and long rehabilitation, he had missed the work he'd done for the intelligence agency. The constant sense of danger. The adrenaline rushes. The euphoria a successful operation provided.

Those had been like a drug to him. He hadn't been aware of that until he'd been forced into withdrawal.

Most of all, however, especially during those first bitter months while he was adjusting to the loss of his hand, as well as dealing with his guilt, he had missed feeling that he was part of something important. Vital. Noble.

That wasn't a word any member of the External Security Team would ever have used to describe what they did. Nor would he. Not then.

Only in retrospect. What they had done for this country had been noble, even if it had also been covert and without any official sanction.

That was why he had jumped at the chance Griff offered him to be part of The Phoenix Brotherhood. It wasn't the same, but it was near enough that it had filled the emptiness being forced out of the CIA had created within him.

"We both knew people who lived that way," he said. "None that were on the wrong side of the law, however."

"You miss it," she said, reading that in his voice. And for some reason, she sounded surprised.

"I did. But working with Griff again—and with the others—it's been…almost the same."

A lifesaver. That was the phrase that had come into his head. He had rejected it, of course. Too melodramatic. Self-pitying. On his lowest days, and he would admit to having had more than a few of those, he had consciously rejected those emotions.

"I lost Paul on that last mission," Andrea said. "You lost everything. I don't think I've ever thought about what happened in those terms."

Duncan said nothing because he couldn't think of anything that wouldn't sound curt. Ungracious. Cruel. He had never intended to reveal to anyone, least of all to Paul Sorrenson's wife, what he had lost during that mission.

"I've made you very uncomfortable," she said, smiling at him again. "I apologize. No more excursions into the past. Not for either of us. Deal?"

"I think that might be wise."

"What you think is that it might be safe," she said. "There's a difference."

For a moment neither of them said anything. Finally Duncan broke the silence, which had definitely not been companionable, like those that fall occasionally between old friends.

"I'll call you if I hear anything from Griff. Until I do, I should finish up the job I was sent here to do. And I want to touch base with the police about anything they might have found out in their investigation. Of course, with the way this was done…" He shrugged, then lifted his suit coat off the chair he'd draped it over.

When he glanced up, he realized she was still watching him with that unspoken concern. It was a look he had seen far too often during the last five years. Never before in her eyes.

At least they had moved away from the personal. Back into territory that was definitely safer, to borrow her word. He slipped his coat on and started down the hall that led to the front door with Andrea trailing him.

"Even smart criminals slip up," he said. "Little things they never think about may give them away."

Meaningless small talk. As inane as it was, it was better than facing the chasm that had loomed before them only seconds ago. He felt the same sense of relief as when he'd entered this house and realized there was nothing of Paul left within it. Nothing he would be forced to confront. Nothing except Paul's wife.

"At least let me feed you dinner," Andrea said.

He turned, his left hand already on the knob of the door. "I'll probably just get room service."

Lunch had been hard enough, although he had been careful to order something he had been confident he could handle. A form of vanity, but it was always easier to eat alone.

"I really *can* cook. No matter what Paul told you." She was smiling at him again.

He wondered what she would do if he told her the truth about how her husband had died. The smile would fade, but at least he could be sure there would be no more invitations to dinner.

"Some other time," he said.

He opened the door, stepping out in the fall sunshine, with a sense of escape as profound as any he'd ever experienced. He took a deep breath, knowing how close that had been.

It would be so damn easy to justify telling her. And in this case, confession would definitely be good for the soul.

His soul, and not hers. Except this was his burden. And it was not one she deserved to ever have to share.

HE HAD ALWAYS HATED the plastic key cards all the hotels used now. Hated them even before he'd lost his hand. With the prices they charged, it seemed they could at least provide you with a damn key.

Like the brochure Andrea had handed him this morning, the credit-card-shaped plastic rectangle was thin enough and slick enough to present a challenge in threading it into the narrow slot. And since using the flimsy card to actually open the door required two hands, he always ended up with his hands crossed, using the left to insert the card and the prosthesis to push down the handle, just as he was now.

Not a problem, really, but an unwanted reminder. And a damned unnecessary one, he decided angrily, as the door to his room swung open.

He was surprised to find the room was pitch-black. Usually when the maids came to clean, they pulled the blackout drapes aside, allowing the sunlight in. Of course, it was late enough now that there wasn't any.

He'd made a couple of detours after he'd left Andrea's. One had been to drive by and take a look at Blackheart, Inc. from the outside. There was nothing remarkable about the building or the location, other than the obvious fact that the firm was doing very well.

The other had been a trip to the public library, where he had used the microfiche files from the local papers to do some research on both Blackheart and Bill Helms. Unlike his street tour of Blackheart's establishment, that side trip had proven interesting. At least it had given him somewhere to begin.

Finally, on his way up, he had stopped by the desk to ask them to fax the material Helms had provided him with to Griff. All that had taken long enough that night had fallen.

With nothing more than a fleeting mental question about the unexpected darkness, he flipped the light switch beside the door. And still felt no sense of alarm when nothing happened.

He couldn't remember turning off the lamp the switch controlled, but maybe he had. Or maybe the bulb had burned out. Maybe that's what the maids had done—left the curtains closed against the chill and turned the lamp on.

He stepped across the hall to reach the next nearest light, which was the one in the bathroom. It was not until it, too, failed to come on when he pressed it, that realization hit him. By then it was already too late.

The blow that struck the back of his head was vicious enough to send him to his knees. There was no pain. Not immediately. There was a blinding numbness, instead, although on some level he was aware of how hard he'd been hit.

And then, as if his body belonged to someone else, he fell forward, his cheek coming to rest against the rough texture of the carpet. That sensation was the last thing he would be aware of for a very long time.

Chapter Three

"Time to wake up, Mr. Culhane."

The voice seemed to come from a distance. And although each of the words made sense individually, Duncan couldn't quite make his mind grasp the point of them.

Not until fingers roughly gripped his chin and shoved his head up. It lolled back bonelessly, striking whatever was behind him. It would have fallen forward again if those fingers had not held it upright.

As he groped toward consciousness, he became aware of the pain in his head. Not the dull ache of a headache, but a pulsing agony that originated in his neck and radiated throughout the bones of his skull. Even his eyes hurt.

It took a second or two to realize that was because he had tried to obey the command by slitting them open. Given the intensity of the light that was shining directly in his face, a slit was all he could manage.

He turned his head, attempting to escape both the brightness and the controlling fingers. He succeeded in the latter—at least briefly. Then the hand that had been holding his chin struck him, slapping his cheek hard enough to turn his head back toward the light.

Whatever was wrong with the muscles at the back of his neck protested the violence of the motion. The discomfort was quickly forgotten, however, when the first blow was followed by another from the same hand, striking his face this time from the opposite direction.

His lip split with the force of the backhand, but he was almost disinterested in the sensation. It was lost among the more powerfully unpleasant ones.

"Wake up, you bastard," the voice demanded again, employing a cheerful, almost singsong tone this time.

Duncan tried to concentrate on remembering if he had ever heard it before. He couldn't, but perhaps that was because he couldn't get his mind to hold long enough to make an identification. The knowledge that he needed to slid out of his head, like rain off a steep roof.

"Open your eyes, Culhane. Do it now."

He wanted to obey, if for no other reason than to avoid the abrupt snap and twist of his aching neck when they hit him again, but he was equally reluctant to face that blinding light. He tried to lift his hand to use as a shield and found that he couldn't move his arms. It scared the hell out of him.

Clawing his way out of the mental fog, he discovered that his wrists had been tied to the arms of the chair in which he was sitting. The one in his room? Or had they transported him somewhere else while he'd been unconscious?

It seemed that might be an important thing to know.

And so, moving as slowly as he dared, he lowered his head slightly, looking out from under his lashes.

Flashlight. He made the identification in the fraction of a second he had managed to keep his eyes open. Someone was pointing the beam directly at his face. And it was very close.

Despite his disorientation, he understood the purpose of that. It effectively prevented him from seeing the face of his assailant. Someone he would recognize? Or someone who planned to leave him alive and didn't want him to be able to furnish the police with a description?

Please, God, he prayed, as the realization of his helplessness began to dawn. *Please, God, let it be that.*

"Who sent you here?"

He couldn't make sense of the question. *He* hadn't been sent. They had come to him. They had been waiting in his hotel room.

He wanted to say that, but his lips didn't seem to work any better than his clouded brain. And then, suddenly, he understood what they meant. They wanted to know who had sent him to San Francisco. But if he told them that—

"We can do this easy," the voice said, low and clearly menacing, "or we can do it hard. The choice is yours."

It was the kind of dialogue he might have expected in a gangster movie. B-grade. Too melodramatic to be taken seriously.

Still, because he knew exactly how painful "doing it hard" could be, he felt a reactive tightening of his stomach muscles, the bone-chilling coldness of dread

building deep inside. That familiar flood of adrenaline, the one that he had just this afternoon thought
of as being addictive, began to pour through his
bloodstream. The only thing it made him feel now
was nauseated.

"A friend," he managed to say. He ran his tongue
over his lips, tasting his own blood, and forced himself to look into the light. "A friend asked me to
come." That breathless quality didn't sound like his
voice. And enunciating the words hurt his damaged
lip. "She needed some help."

"Mrs. Sorrenson."

It had not been a question, but he nodded agreement. There was no use denying what they knew.
That would only make them angry. If this bastard
knew Andrea's name, then he knew about their relationship. Exactly how much he knew—

"Except you were in town *before* she called you."

They could have found out easily enough when
he'd checked in. Whether or not that meant they also
knew what he had been working on before Andrea
called him...

"I had another client," he said.

Tell them just enough to stay alive. That had always
been the rule. And they had all understood where the
line was to be drawn.

"In your capacity as security consultant, of
course."

There was a sardonic familiarity about the tone,
which nibbled at the rim of his memory. *Blackheart?*
The timbre of this voice seemed remarkably similar.
Or maybe it was the mockery he was reacting to.

The words themselves were the same ones Helms

had used this afternoon. And the only people who had heard them…

He nodded, moving his head carefully. He had learned that if he kept very still, the pain in his skull eased to a dull rage.

"And the *name* of your previous client, Mr. Culhane?"

Beyond the line.

"Privileged information," Duncan said, trying to brace himself mentally for what would happen.

There was a small, almost soundless breath of laughter. Again all the muscles in his stomach clenched, just as they always did when he reached the top of a roller coaster. Knowing what was coming. Anticipating it with a certain resigned desperation.

The light moved, jerking upward almost faster than his eyes could follow. When it descended, the head of the heavy flashlight smashed down with a stunning force against the unprotected fingers of his left hand.

He managed to swallow the howl of pain and outrage, but he couldn't prevent the shocked gasp from echoing outward, followed by a low, guttural moan as the pain roared up his arm. He clamped his teeth into his bottom lip as soon as he realized that almost bestial sound had come from his mouth.

"Painful?" the voice asked.

The sarcasm had been replaced by a patently false solicitousness that made Duncan determined not to react the next time. Small satisfaction, but then small satisfactions were all he was likely to have in this situation.

"You've got only the one, you know," the voice reminded, the tone one might use to a not-very-bright child. "It would be tragic if something...permanently debilitating happened to it. Highly inconvenient for daily living, I'd imagine. So... Shall we try this again?"

For a second, Duncan thought he meant another blow from the flashlight. Then, in the midst of the uncontrollable wash of terror that created, he realized his captor was asking him once more for the name of his previous client.

Could they possibly know? Would they know if he lied? And if they did, would he be any worse off? Could he be?

"Crierson Biotec," he said, trying to prepare himself mentally for the crushing impact of the flashlight against his knuckles in case he had guessed wrong about the extent of their knowledge.

His fingers had attempted to recoil after the last blow, seeking some means of escape. He had discovered that in addition to the restraints placed around his wrists, something had been strapped over the ends of his fingers, fastening them down as well. Although he couldn't be certain, it felt as if they had been taped to the arm of the chair.

Duct tape? That ubiquitous miracle of modern science, with its thousand and one uses. The strong-as-steel silver tape had been standard equipment on team missions. You never knew when it would come in handy.

His mind tightly and deliberately focused on those memories, he waited for the next blow to fall. And waited. And waited.

Long enough that finally he was forced to draw a

shuddering breath. Too damned audible in the quiet darkness.

"How do you know Mrs. Sorrenson?"

Risk another lie? Or a partial truth?

As much of the truth as you can tell, Griff had taught his team. *That way it's easier to remember exactly what you've said when you've reached the ends of your endurance.*

Duncan knew from past experience that he wasn't nearly at that point. Not anywhere close.

"Her husband and I were friends."

"Her *late* husband."

"Yes."

He took another breath, grateful they hadn't hit him again. That gratitude could be dangerous. Seductive, even. It made you want to please your interrogators. That and the pain.

"A purely personal relationship?"

With Paul? Or with Andrea? He supposed it didn't matter.

"Yes."

"And because of your friendship, she asked you to recover her grandmother's stolen property?"

"Yes."

"Purely for personal reasons?"

"Yes."

There was a long pause. Somewhere from across the room Duncan heard a whisper of movement, although the light directed at his eyes never wavered.

How many of them were there? he wondered. At least two. He realized he had known that from the beginning, although he wasn't sure how he had known. The sound of their breathing?

"I wonder why it is I don't believe you, Mr. Culhane?"

This time when the light began its upward swing, Duncan tried to keep his eyes focused on the blackness behind it. Tried not to think about what was going to happen. Tried to glimpse a face during that long heartbeat before the head of the heavy flashlight slammed down on his fingers again, rendering him incapable of any further thought.

He didn't succeed in penetrating the darkness behind the light. Not any more than he had succeeded in preventing the gasp of shock and unspeakable rage. If he ever got his hands on this bastard...

And somewhere in the most primitive part of his mind, down in the place where the primeval nightmare fears hide, the word repeated. Echoing over and over again.

Hands. And in his case—

"Who are you?" the voice demanded, all pretense of mockery or concern erased.

"Duncan Culhane," he said, the words sounding even more thready than the first had been. "My name is Duncan Culhane. I don't know what the hell you want from me. Why are you asking me these questions?"

Again he heard the breath of laughter. It infuriated him to know that they were laughing at him. Not so much, however, as what followed it.

"Maybe Mrs. Sorrenson will be more willing to answer them. Women don't like to have things turn messy. Or painful," the voice added, obviously relishing the threat.

Andrea.

"I've answered your questions, you bastard," Duncan said, spitting out the words in a rage he didn't have to pretend. Not now. "Andrea Sorrenson is an old friend. She asked me for a favor. Whatever you're trying to make out of that is just that. Something you're trying to make up."

He had finally come out of his mental fog enough to realize that his initial reaction had been a mistake. Disoriented, he hadn't displayed the sense of outrage and terror a normal person would feel on being attacked, held prisoner, tortured.

He had reacted as his training demanded. He had tried to think his way through the minefield of the questions, despite the fact that his head felt as if it had already exploded.

He should have cried. Screamed at the top of his lungs the first time they'd hit him. Cursed them. Maybe if he had—

In the midst of that self-castigation, someone pounded on the door to his room. Duncan jumped, reacting in his vulnerability to that unexpected sound.

Not the flashlight, he reassured himself. Relief that it wasn't coursed through his body as he identified the sound. *Somebody was knocking at the door.*

Somebody *they* weren't expecting. He knew that, because he could sense their shocked stillness. The almost subliminal sounds of their breathing had been suspended. As was his. All of them were listening intently.

The disembodied voice from the other side of the door called out, "Room service, Mr. Culhane. I've got your sandwich."

The other thing he had done when he'd stopped by

the desk to send his fax. He'd asked them to have room service send up a club sandwich and a pot of coffee. And a normal person would react to this situation—

"Help!" he bellowed at the top of his lungs. "Get security! There's somebody in my room. I've been attacked."

The flashlight swung sideways this time, slamming with the same vicious force against his temple. His head fell forward, a wave of blackness engulfing him.

He tried to fight it. Struggled to stay awake. And failed. The last sound he heard was the unmistakable crash of pottery from the hallway outside his room.

ANDREA REALIZED THAT SHE'D put her hand around the receiver a half dozen times since Duncan left the house this afternoon. She almost wished she didn't know where he was staying, so the temptation to call him wouldn't be so damn strong. She could, after all, think of a dozen perfectly legitimate reasons to call. *Perfectly* legitimate.

Except she had never been very good at self-deception. Every time she found herself reaching for the phone, she had also found enough pride to keep her hand from completing the motion.

She would have thought that he might have called her by now. He or Griff. Maybe they figured that if they didn't have anything to report—

Startled, she raised her eyes from the book she'd been trying to read, listening for a repetition of the sound she'd heard. She sat in breathless stillness as long as she could, but there was nothing else.

A limb rubbing against the house, she reassured

herself. She lowered her gaze to the page, trying to make the disconnected marks on it assume coherence. After a moment, her attention still unwillingly focused toward the back of the house, whatever she had heard before came again. She closed the book carefully, and still listening, laid it on the table beside her chair.

She had lived here alone for the last five years, and she couldn't remember feeling the least bit nervous. Maybe the approaching storm had charged the air with an undercurrent of electricity, but suddenly, inexplicably, she was filled with anxiety.

She rose and moved as silently as she could across the room. Simply because it had been there when he died, Paul's gun was still in the drawer of the bedside table. Feeling ridiculous that she had thought of it, she hurried along the dark hall toward the bedroom.

Since there was no one else living in the house, she didn't keep the drawer locked. In only a matter of seconds she held the semiautomatic in her hand.

And as soon as her fingers had wrapped around the stock, she felt a surge of adrenaline. The old flight or fight syndrome. Except she didn't have any place to run to.

She wrapped both hands around the weapon, the left supporting the right, just as she had been taught. She held it out before her, making her way back down the hall to the kitchen and then across it to the backdoor.

The curtains had been drawn over the glass panels that comprised the top half. She resisted the urge to pull them aside and look out. Instead, she leaned against the wall beside the door, her gun still held in firing position, and listened.

Whatever had been out there before wasn't making noise now. The only sound in the darkness was her own breathing.

She edged closer to the door, trying to look through the narrow opening where the curtains didn't quite come together. Although her view was limited, everything seemed normal in her small backyard.

The moonlight was clear and revealing. Nothing there that shouldn't be. Nothing that wasn't well-known and familiar.

She drew a breath of relief, but almost before the action was complete, she heard the same faint noise she had heard before. This time it seemed to have moved around to the side of the house.

She glanced toward the phone, tempted to call 911. Her justification for doing so seemed pretty thin. ''I hear a noise in my backyard'' wouldn't make much of an impression on a harried police dispatcher.

She couldn't even decide why this was spooking her. She wasn't the kind who rushed to get a gun every time she heard something strange.

And then, almost with a sense of vindication, she heard a sound she recognized. Someone ran across the deck outside the sun porch, feet pounding against the wooden boards. There was no attempt at stealth.

She pushed the curtain aside and watched a dark figure flee through the broken patterns of moonlight and shadow on the lawn, heading toward the back of her lot. There was nothing there but the low hedge which marked her property line. Behind it a sloping hillside led down to a densely wooded area. Once he reached that—

Her left hand had already started toward the dead bolt before she forced her fingers to stop. She'd be an idiot to go outside. Even if there was a chance she might get a glimpse of whoever had been lurking around or of the vehicle he'd driven up here. And there probably *wasn't* a chance.

She was safe as long as she stayed inside the house. Paul used to call this Fort Sorrenson because of the security measures he'd had installed, although they were across the continent from his connections to the CIA.

After his death, she'd been grateful that he'd been so careful. Of course, given what Paul had done for a living—

A man's profile, a silhouette against the lesser darkness of the night, appeared in front of the pane of glass she had been looking through. She stumbled backward, trying to get away from the door. As she did, she put her left hand under the right and pointed the muzzle of the semiautomatic directly at that panel.

Smooth squeeze, Andy. Don't jerk it. She could hear Paul's voice in her head. *Just keep squeezing until you run out of ammo.*

Her finger had already begun to tighten over the trigger when whoever was out there turned, putting his hand along his forehead and leaning against the glass to peer inside the kitchen. He was too close for the moonlight to be much help in making an identification, but still, there was an indefinable something...

Her finger released its tension. She allowed the

hand holding the gun to fall to her side as she ran back to the door she had just deserted. Her fingers fumbled with the night latch. When the bolt was free of the frame, she turned the knob, throwing open the door.

"Duncan?" Then, seeing him more clearly, she said his name again. And this time the tone of it was entirely different. "Oh, my God, *Duncan.*"

"YOU MUST HAVE SCARED him away."

She finished her recital, at the same time dabbing at the cut on his mouth with a cotton ball she'd dampened with alcohol. She stepped back, taking his chin in her hand to turn his face toward the bathroom light. He flinched, closing his eyes as if the brightness hurt them.

"I think you may have a concussion," she said.

He wouldn't even talk about going to the emergency room. It had been a struggle to get him to let her do anything about his injuries. And what she had finally been allowed to do hadn't been much.

"It won't be the first."

As he said that, he put the inside of his left wrist against the back of his neck, turning his head slowly from side to side as if he were trying to stretch cramped muscles. He closed his eyes and took a couple of deep breaths as he did.

"And you really don't have any idea what those men in your room wanted?"

He lowered his hand and looked up, still squinting. He started to shake his head, and then he winced.

"Bastards," he said softly. "I'm not sure *they*

knew what they were after. Other than a little recreation.''

''What does that mean?''

''If they know who I am, then they would also know our relationship. Why waste time asking questions? And if they *didn't* know about our ties to the agency, then why pull something like that in the first place? What could they hope to gain? It doesn't make sense. Other than they just like to hurt people. Like to play at being tough.''

''I'm not sure I'd call that playing,'' she said.

Her eyes fell to the bruised and swollen fingers of the hand he was now holding, chest high, cradled in the palm of the right. As soon as he realized she was looking at it, he put both hands in his lap. Her eyes lifted back to his.

''If they were really that interested in making me talk,'' Duncan said, ''there are more efficient ways.''

She didn't want to imagine what those might be. ''You think they're the same people who stole Helms's collection?''

''Why come after me? They got away with what they wanted. Why make themselves vulnerable? Why not just lie low and enjoy their success?''

''Because they see you as a threat,'' Andrea suggested.

''I haven't proven to be much of one. Besides, supposedly only two people know I'm looking into that robbery. Helms and Blackheart.''

''You think it was one of them?'' she asked incredulously. ''You think Helms or Blackheart sent those men?''

"Probably not. They're both supposed to be bright. This wasn't. Somehow…" He let the word trail, again unconsciously cupping his hand against his chest.

"If you aren't going to have that X-rayed, at least let me put some ice on it," she said. "To keep down the swelling."

It was probably too late for that, but it was all she knew to do. That and offer him some over-the-counter pain reliever she had already put out on the vanity.

"Okay," he said, sounding resigned.

He stood, suddenly filling all the space in the small bathroom. Seated on the john, he had seemed almost vulnerable. Now he was once again subtly and yet undoubtedly in charge, despite his injuries.

They were close enough that she became aware of the scent of his body. It was undeniably masculine. The starch the laundry had put in that white button-down. A hint of after shave or cologne—something as understated as Duncan himself. The sharpness of the alcohol she'd just applied.

Without moving, they stood facing one another for several long seconds. She was between him and the door. It had been her suggestion to head back to the kitchen, so it was definitely her move.

And the only one she wanted to make was to step forward. To lean her cheek against Duncan's chest and feel his arms close around her, holding her tight. Keeping her safe.

She wondered how he would respond if she did. Although his initial reaction would probably be tell-ing, she wasn't sure she was up to facing that particular revelation tonight. Because if he *didn't* put his arms around her...

She took an involuntary breath at the thought of that painful possibility. It broke the spell that had held them motionless. He shifted his weight, clearly conveying that he was anxious to move. And so, without saying any of the things she wanted to say to him, she turned, leading the way to the other room.

AFTER SHE HAD CRUSHED ICE in the food processor, she put the pieces in the middle of a clean dish towel, folding it lengthwise. She carried it over to the breakfast bar where Duncan was sitting.

His head was down, his eyes seeming to study the strutted, discolored fingers of his left hand, which lay palm up on the counter in front of him. The right, the artificial one, was hidden in his lap.

And for the first time she realized why they had targeted his hand. She supposed she was slow, but doing something like that took a certain kind of mentality. Thankfully it was one she didn't have.

She wondered what he'd been thinking while they were doing whatever they had done to his hand. His *only* hand. And then knew she couldn't possibly understand what he had felt.

Just as she couldn't understand people who would do something like this. The same cold-blooded cruelty that had victimized her grandparents' generation all across Europe.

They just like to hurt people. Like to play at being tough. An apt description.

Duncan didn't look up as she approached. She

slipped her fingers under his wrist, lifting it. He glanced up then, his eyes focusing on her face.

They stayed there, watching it rather than what she was doing. She wrapped the towel around his hand, placing the ice under the battered knuckles and pulling the ends of the cloth around it, lapping them over one another in his palm. Only then did his gaze fall.

"Can you hold it?" she asked.

He answered by putting his thumb over the crossed ends, securing the makeshift ice pack.

She had already begun to turn away, when he said, his voice so low she almost didn't catch the words, "I was terrified."

She turned back, swallowing against the hard, aching knot that tightened her throat. Tears threatened, stinging behind her eyes, but she refused to let them fall. She would never do that to him.

Perhaps her very stillness gave her away. He looked up, something in his eyes she'd never seen there before. A speechless rage and a vulnerability she could never have imagined seeing in Duncan Culhane's eyes.

He was the toughest man she'd ever known. Even Paul had commented on his seeming inability to feel fear, no matter how desperate the situation. And now…

She couldn't think of a single thing to say in response. She knew it had taken enormous courage to make that confession. She wouldn't demean it by offering some ridiculous platitude in return. Or by trying to comfort him, as if he were a child, afraid of the dark.

He'd had a right to be terrified. She would have been. Any sane person in that situation would have been.

She nodded instead of speaking, holding his eyes until they fell again to his damaged hand. She watched a muscle in his jaw tighten and then release, working under the sun-bronzed skin and late-day shadow of beard that was as dark as his hair.

And then she watched her fingers reach out and touch his chin, aware this time of the texture of his whiskers against their sensitive tips. He didn't resist when she lifted his head slightly, turning it toward her.

There was a question in his eyes, but she made no attempt to answer it. Instead, for once in their long relationship, she simply followed her instincts. If he could find the courage to confess that very legitimate terror, then surely she could find a courage to match it.

After all, hers was only a fear of rejection. One that had allowed him to disappear from her life once before because she hadn't dared to tell him how she felt. She had decided, even before Griff returned her call, that she wouldn't let that happen again.

She lowered her head, her mouth settling, as weightless as breath, over the bruised lips. There was a second's hesitation before they responded. Long enough for her to feel fear stir in her heart. And then, slowly, they parted under hers.

For a moment she wasn't sure if that was from surprise or if Duncan was indeed returning her kiss. That uncertainty was fleeting as well. Only until his tongue invaded, challenging hers with a hunger that matched her own. A need that seemed to exceed it.

And she didn't care if he needed her only for tonight. Or if his kiss were only in response to her unspoken offer of a warm, living body beside him to stave off the coldness of his remembered fear.

All she cared about was that after ten years, Duncan Culhane's arms closed around her, finally drawing her into an embrace she had only dreamed about.

Chapter Four

"There's something I have to tell you," Duncan said, his breath feathering over her throat. "Something—"

"No," she denied, pulling back from his embrace to put her fingers over his lips.

She had been expecting this. It hadn't come until they'd reached the bedroom. Of course, there hadn't been time for a lot of conversation. Their mouths had been in constant contact throughout the slow journey down the hall.

"Whatever you think you need to tell me, Duncan, I don't want to hear it. Not now."

He wanted to confess the guilt he felt for her husband's death. A totally unjustified guilt, according to Griff. And although she acknowledged there would have to be a time for them to talk about Paul, what was happening between them now wasn't about death. It was about life. Their lives.

She had faithfully fulfilled every vow she had made to Paul. At the time she had made them, standing beside him at the altar, she had truly believed that she'd put what she felt for Duncan behind her. She had been Paul's wife, in every sense of the word and to the best of her ability. And she had loved him.

Just not like this.

Not with this long-delayed passion and excitement. Her love for Paul had been grounded in respect and friendship. Not a lesser love, perhaps, but a different one.

She removed her fingers from Duncan's lips and began to unfasten the buttons down the front of his shirt. Not simply because she wanted the sensual pleasure of undressing him—which she did—but because she wasn't sure he would be able to manage them on his own.

He watched her, his eyes following the downward motion of her hands until they pushed the unbuttoned shirt apart, revealing a white cotton-knit undershirt. Her fingers found the buckle of his belt, making quick work of that, too, before moving on to the zipper of his slacks.

Finally she was able to slip her hands under the hem of the T-shirt, her palms gliding over the hard warmth of his stomach. There wasn't an ounce of excess flesh on his body. The skin was firm and very smooth except for the arrow of coarse hair that centered it.

Her hands trailed upward, moving over his ribs and on to the cleanly delineated muscles of his chest. When she touched his nipples, his breathing hesitated and was then sharply indrawn—almost a gasp. Emboldened, she lifted the undershirt with her thumbs, lowering her head to run her tongue over one of the small, hardened nubs.

"Andrea."

"Shh," she said, her breath so near the moisture she'd left on his skin that he shivered. "Don't talk. Please, Duncan, just for tonight. Just...don't talk."

"You don't understand."

"I understand everything that matters," she said. "As for the rest..."

The words were lost as her lips closed around his nipple, suckling strongly. His response was all she might have hoped for. Everything she'd waited for through these long years. Even when she had not been aware that this—and he—were what she awaited.

He bent, gathering her in his arms. When they'd left the den, she had guided him to the guest room. She didn't want any possibility that she had been Paul's wife, that she had lived with him in this house, to interfere with what was happening tonight. Not for him. And not for her.

Instead of laying her on the coverlet as she'd expected, Duncan set her down on her feet beside the bed. He took a step back, his eyes luminescent in the dimness. Anxiety building, she looked up at him, trying to hold on to what had been in them only seconds ago.

"I can't..." he began, and her heart stopped. She saw the breath he drew, lifting his shoulders, before he finished. "I don't think I can undress you."

Her relief was so great her knees went weak. "I can probably manage that on my own," she said, smiling at him.

There was no answering movement of his lips. His face in the shadows was almost stern.

"That isn't the way I've always imagined this

would be," he said softly. "Not the way I *wanted* it to be."

She nodded, holding his eyes, again fighting for emotional control. And then the sense of what he had just said hit her.

That isn't the way I've always imagined this would be. No matter how many times she replayed the phrase in her consciousness, there was only one possible interpretation.

"*Did* you imagine it?"

"Almost from the day I met you," he said. His lips moved, the tilt too subtle to be called a smile.

"It's taken you a damn long time to let me know."

The silence lasted long enough to become uncomfortable before he broke it. "I thought it wouldn't be fair."

"Fair?"

"Considering the risks inherent in what we did for Griff."

None of them had married. Not until the team had been dissolved. No one except Paul. And in the end...

"I thought..." She paused, shaking her head, the motion small and tight. "I thought there were other reasons. I always wondered if I had told you how I felt—"

"How *you* felt?" he repeated.

He hadn't known, she realized. All these years, he really hadn't known.

"Almost from the day I met you," she said, deliberately echoing his words.

"Then... What about Paul?"

There was probably nothing she could say that

wouldn't make him think less of her for that. She had questioned her own motives a thousand times.

"I thought what we had would be enough," she said simply.

That was true, although it offered no defense of what she had done. And there were defenses. Maybe none that mattered, but still—

"I killed him."

The words she hadn't wanted to hear—had hoped he wouldn't say tonight—were suddenly in the darkness between them. A living, breathing force.

"I know you feel that you were somehow responsible—" she began, thinking about what Griff had told her.

"I don't *feel* responsible, Andrea. *I* killed him. I'm the one who killed Paul. Not figuratively. *Literally* killed him. That's what I've been trying to tell you. I killed your husband."

The sense of what he was saying finally broke through her preconceptions, changing everything she had thought she understood.

"You mean...with your own hands?" she whispered.

The muscle in his jaw tightened again, and then released. "With my own hand," he repeated softly.

She couldn't know what was in her face. Given what was suddenly in her head, however...

After a moment, he took another step back. Away from her. Moving into the shadow cast by the high post of the bed. And this time she did nothing to stop him. Finally he turned and crossed the bedroom, closing the door behind him, leaving her alone. More alone than she had ever been in her life.

"YOU NEED TO GET SOMEONE out here to take over."

"You said you weren't seriously hurt. Andrea's all right, so—"

"That isn't the point," Duncan broke in savagely. "Whatever you're playing at in putting us together, Griff, it's over. Done. Enough is enough."

"I don't *have* anybody else," Griff said, not bothering to deny the accusation. "And I won't have for at least a couple of days."

Duncan briefly considered whether or not he could believe that. That he did showed the strain he'd been under during the last twelve hours, he admitted reluctantly. Because Cabot had never lied to him. Not in the entire time he'd worked for him. It would be as foreign to their relationship as a betrayal.

"I don't want Andrea left alone," Griff went on. "Not after what you've just told me. I'll get someone else out to the coast as soon as possible. I promise you. As soon as I can."

Duncan's injured hand tightened convulsively, and painfully, around the phone. It seemed he had no choice. Until someone was on the scene to take over this assignment, it was up to him to figure out what was going on. And more importantly, up to him to insure that, even if he couldn't get the music box back, whoever had been lurking around Andrea's house tonight wouldn't make a return visit.

"Anything on Blackheart?" he asked instead of answering Griff's appeal. Cabot knew him well enough to understand that he wouldn't leave until he'd been relieved. "I did a little research on my own yesterday. Only what's public, so I know about his former occupation. I've been thinking that maybe this was a preretirement heist. One final nose-thumbing at the authorities. He seems to have excelled at that kind of thing.''

''He's been clean for a long time,'' Griff said. ''We've already considered most of the information available about Blackheart's current operation, which caters to a very wealthy clientele. It doesn't appear he's ever tried to hide his past, not from them or from anyone.''

''That may not mean he doesn't have something to hide.''

There was a beat of silence. ''On the other hand,'' Griff said, and left the word hanging between them.

In Duncan's head, he heard his own confession. *With my own hand.*

''Yeah?''

''It seems John Patrick Blackheart has a son. Illegitimate. Never acknowledged.''

''And?'' Duncan probed, trying to understand how that might have relevance for this case.

''Michael Blackheart was just released from prison.''

''For robbery?'' Duncan asked sharply.

''He was a cat burglar. Apparently following in his father's footsteps.''

''Where is he now?'' Duncan asked, reassessing his reactions to the men who had attacked him last night.

He had thought the voice coming from the darkness behind that flashlight might be Blackheart's. There had been something different enough about it, however, that he'd eventually decided his response must be rooted in a reaction to the mockery of its tone rather than in any real similarity to the security expert's voice. Was it possible that a son's voice might be enough like his father's to have triggered that haunting sense of familiarity?

"We don't know. We're trying to find out. We're also trying to cross match the items that were taken against those that have been reported missing since the war. The problem is there had to be someone left to report them."

"A survivor like Andrea's grandmother."

"Who, by the way, never posted the Lalique to any of the lists of missing artworks that have been compiled. Maybe she didn't know about them, although they've gotten a lot of media play and word-of-mouth in the international Jewish community."

"Maybe she didn't have any hope of ever seeing her music box again," Duncan suggested. "Or anything else that had been taken from her family."

"There are probably others who feel the same way. That will make what we're trying to do from this end more difficult." There was a small silence, and then Griff changed the subject. "Can you tell us anything else about the men who attacked you?"

Every time I move, Duncan thought. *Something short and very descriptive.* Which wasn't what Griff was looking for.

"I never saw them. Nobody saw them. By the time the busboy got back with hotel security, they were gone."

"Impressions?"

"They enjoyed it," Duncan said. "Based on their questions, I'm not sure they were looking for information as much as looking to intimidate. I think I'm supposed to just pack up and leave San Francisco in the morning.''

Another silence, and belatedly Duncan realized that's exactly what he'd just asked Griff to allow him do.

''What happened in that hotel room has nothing to do with my asking for a replacement,'' he said, feeling defensive, even though this was Griff, who should know him better than that.

''I never thought it did,'' Cabot assured him calmly. And then, after another silence, ''Have you told Andrea what really happened in Iraq?''

Trust Cabot to cut straight to the heart.

''I've told her the *truth*,'' he said.

It was probably obvious by his tone that he didn't want to talk about this. He hoped to hell it was.

Griff let the subject drop. ''I'll call you if we get anything definitive on the missing items. Or on anything else. Until we do—''

''I'll be here,'' Duncan said shortly.

He punched the off button with his thumb, the only finger it didn't hurt to move, and flipped the phone closed. When he turned around, Andrea was standing in the doorway, again watching him.

''There's more to it than that,'' she said.

''More to what?''

He laid the phone on the island, and put his hand down on top of the impromptu ice pack she'd fixed. It seemed as if hours had passed since then, but the ice was still rigid and frozen in the middle of the towel.

''To Paul's death.''

''I thought you didn't want to talk about that.''

He wasn't up to this. He had known it was a mistake to respond to her kiss, but when her lips touched his, as soft and warm as he had always imagined they would be, he hadn't been able to summon the strength to resist.

"I didn't. Not then. But now that you *have* talked about it—"

"Let it go, Andrea. What happened a few minutes ago was mistake. Thankfully not an irreparable one."

"Are you talking about what happened between us?"

"*Nothing* happened between us. Nothing but a few kisses. And a long overdue confession. Let's leave it at that."

"Exactly *which* confession would that be, Duncan?"

Why the hell couldn't he have kept his mouth shut for one more night. You would think that after all these years of *not* telling her how he felt about her—

"The one about Paul's death," he said.

"If what you told me is true, then I think I have to know why. I *deserve* to know. You can't say something like that and then just decide you aren't going to explain."

"I'm *not* going to explain. What happened on that mission is still, as far as I'm aware, classified."

"And you swore an oath never to divulge any of it?"

"Something like that," he said.

She laughed. "The famous national security defense. Did you guys have some kind of ceremony? Some kind of blood brother crap? Or did Griff just tap you on the shoulder with his magic sword and suddenly you're all the sole defenders of the free world?''

"Something like that, too," he said again, his voice as quietly sarcastic as hers had been.

"I want to know how my husband died, damn it."

"No, you don't," he said. "Trust me, Andrea, you really don't."

Maybe because of what was in his voice or his eyes as he said it, it seemed that she finally believed him. This time she was the one who retreated.

After she had disappeared into that dark hallway, his eyes fell again to his hands. He held them out before him. One flesh and blood, seeming, after the events of the last few hours, far too vulnerable, with its network of delicate nerves and tendons and arteries and the fragility of its bone structure.

And the other... A constant reminder, if he had needed one, of something he had known all along. *Almost since the day I met you.*

Andrea Sorrenson wasn't for him. Given who he was and what he had done, she never could be.

"IT'S HELMS," Andrea said.

Duncan opened one eye, and then quickly closed it against the glare of the morning sun, coming in too strongly through the sheer curtains of Andrea's den. He had intended to stay awake and keep watch, but apparently he'd fallen asleep on the leather sofa.

Evidently, keeping watch hadn't been necessary. Everything seemed perfectly normal. The smell of brewing coffee competed with the scent of whatever shampoo Andrea had used during her recent shower.

She had wound a thick white towel turban-style around her head, maybe to answer the phone, and she was wearing a man's navy silk robe, belted at the waist. The cuffs had been turned back a couple of times so that the sleeves wouldn't hang down over her hands. In one of them, she held the phone.

"What does he want?" Duncan asked, the effort at putting words together setting off the ache at the back of his skull.

"He thinks he knows how they did it. He wants you to come down there so he can show you."

"To the Carlyle?"

"To Helms Enterprises. And he doesn't want Blackheart to know he's meeting with you."

"Meaning he suspects Blackheart was in on it?"

"He seems to think the thieves would have had to have help from Blackheart or one of his associates to carry this off."

Since that was the conclusion Duncan had come to yesterday, he nodded, reaching for the phone.

"I told him I'd give you the message," she said.

"He hung up?"

"There was a lot of background noise. People talking. I think he must have been in a meeting."

He nodded again, wondering why it felt as if she weren't telling him everything. Despite last night, there was no reason for Andrea to keep anything about the robbery from him. After all, he was here at her request.

"Any word from Griff?" he asked, wondering about the results of his own request.

"Not this morning. Were you expecting him to call?"

"Not necessarily," he admitted. "I suppose I was hoping he'd found something that would give us a place to start."

"It sounds as if Helms has already done that."

Duncan nodded, wondering what Helms could have turned up that hadn't been equally obvious to Griff's sources within the agency. Unless what Helms thought Duncan should see also had something to do with Blackheart's unacknowledged son. And of course, there was only one way to find out.

"I need a shower," he said.

"I put clean towels on the hamper. Your shirt's in the dryer with a sheet of fabric softener. I didn't think I'd have time to wash it. He wants us there within the hour. Those are his words, not mine, by the way."

"Us?" Duncan asked, picking the salient point out of Helms's high-handed instructions.

"That's what he said. I *do* have a vested interest in this, remember."

Duncan didn't like either of his choices. Take Andrea with him, as per Helms's instructions, which would mean their spending more time together. After last night, that would be uncomfortable for both of them.

Or leave her here alone. Unprotected. Although he still believed his assessment of the men in his room last night was correct, even if their intimidation was simply that, the threat that they might harm Andrea was still effective. And a chance he wasn't willing to take.

"Give me half an hour and a cup of coffee," he suggested, swinging his legs off the couch.

"I THOUGHT YOU SHOULD SEE this," Helms said, using his index finger to push his glasses further up on the bridge of his nose.

When the security guard had conducted them into this utility hallway where Helms was waiting for them, there had been no "Thanks for coming." No pretense at social chitchat. Even Helms's greeting of Andrea had seemed curt and preoccupied.

He was treating Duncan exactly as he would have treated one of his own employees. Obviously the point Duncan had tried to make yesterday, that he worked for Andrea and not for Helms, had been lost on the millionaire. Or maybe this was simply the way he treated everyone.

"What is it?" Duncan asked.

"You'll see," Helms said, pushing open the door and gesturing them to precede him inside an unlighted room.

Andrea went first, and Duncan followed. After last night, he felt a tinge of apprehension about stepping into that darkness. As soon as Helms joined them, however, he touched a switch by the door that threw on the overhead lights.

They were in what was obviously a conference room of some sort. Considering the utilitarian starkness of the hallway outside, the room was both larger and more elaborately decorated than Duncan had expected.

Tables had been set up in a long T, with a tabletop lectern positioned at the front center of the crossbar, making Duncan wonder if this was where the meeting Andrea mentioned hearing in the background of Helms's phone call had occurred. Behind the lectern was a huge screen. Its placement drew Duncan's attention to the opposite wall, where he discovered the expected window for the projection of slides or movies.

Plush leather chairs lined both sides of the tables, providing seating for probably forty or fifty people. On top of one of the row of tables that ran down the center of the room, a gray cloth rested over several objects that appeared to be of differing sizes and shapes.

"These were offered for sale on the international art black market last night," Helms said, walking over and pulling the cloth back to reveal a conglomeration of vases, small paintings and statues.

"From the collection?" Duncan asked.

"I bought them for a fraction of their value. I had hoped that by offering for them, I might be able to get some indication of who was involved in their sale."

"Did you?"

There was a small hesitation before Helms answered. His fingers lingered over an enameled statue that had a slightly oriental look. Duncan tried to place it on the list of stolen items he'd been provided—the one he'd faxed to Griff last night—and couldn't.

"It appears they're more sophisticated than I'd given them credit for."

"You indicated to Mrs. Sorrenson that you know how they pulled off the theft."

Helms's eyes shifted to Andrea's face, holding there a few seconds before they returned to Duncan's. "I think he had inside help."

"He?"

"One thief. Working alone."

"How do you know?" Andrea asked.

"Do you remember the tapes from the surveillance van that Blackheart claimed were blank?"

Duncan nodded, finally understanding why they had been brought to this particular room. "They weren't," he said, willing to play along.

"Not with some technical intervention on our part. It's amazing what computer enhancements can achieve. Even on video tapes which are purported to be blank. It was really rather silly of Blackheart to say that, considering what the business of Helms Enterprises is and always has been."

It was as if Helms thought of himself in the third person, as an entity separate from the rather nondescript man who stood before them. Maybe having as much money as he did made you think that way.

And what he had said was, of course, nothing less than the truth. It *would* be silly to try to put something over on Helms's experts in any area involving technology. The only problem was that however else one might choose to characterize Patrick Blackheart, he wasn't silly. Or stupid.

"I'm surprised he didn't just destroy them," Duncan said.

"It's often surprising what people think they can get away with. I suppose he thought that by erasing the tapes, he would permanently destroy any images they might contain."

Duncan would have thought the same thing. It seemed that enhancement of nothing would still be nothing.

"And…that wasn't the case?" Duncan said.

"Technology is the slave of those who are clever enough and courageous enough to employ it, Mr. Culhane. Would you like to watch?"

Duncan inclined his head in agreement, his eyes meeting Andrea's. Hers were questioning. Obviously she was as surprised as he had been by Helms's claim.

"There's quite a bit of it, actually," Helms went on. "Perhaps you'd be more comfortable if you sat here, Mrs. Sorrenson."

As he made the suggestion, he touched the top of the massive chair at the end of the row of tables. On casters, the chair rolled back easily, despite the thick carpeting. Helms smiled at Andrea, his hand gesturing toward it in invitation.

Her eyes held Duncan's, one brow lifted in inquiry. He nodded, the movement small enough that he hoped it wasn't obvious to their host. When Andrea had been seated, Helms pushed the chair back in, so that she was at the end of the tables, directly in front of the screen. Then Helms turned back to him.

"Mr. Culhane?"

"I'm fine," Duncan said.

For some reason a prickle of unease rifted along his spine. He wasn't the expert Helms was, but the more he thought about this, the more convinced he was that if those security tapes really had been erased, no images could be recovered.

If that were possible, he would have been aware of the process. There would have been whispers of something like that within the security community. Within the CIA, if nowhere else.

He would have heard them. So would Blackheart. Unless this process was so new that Helms's company had developed it and not yet obtained patent protection. If that were the case, Helms wouldn't be eager to show it off before strangers. He didn't seem that trusting.

Duncan's unease increased when the lights in the room dimmed, just as if they were in a theater. Despite his unanswered questions, his eyes were drawn to the screen.

It was immediately obvious something *was* there. Some pattern of light indicated that tape was rolling, but it took a moment for his eyes to adjust to the darkness of the images. And another to begin to make sense of them.

What was playing on the screen in Bill Helms's private projection room wasn't something that had occurred here in San Francisco two nights ago. And it didn't have anything to do with Blackheart, father or son. Or even with the theft of Helms's collection.

As the screen lightened, and the grainy black and white tape, almost like newsreel footage, began to play out above their heads, the same cold wave of sick dread he had felt when his hands had been taped to that chair in his hotel room settled like a rock in Duncan Culhane's stomach.

Because there was no doubt in his mind where this had been shot. And it wasn't in the Southworth auction house. It was in a small, dark room in a prison hellhole in Basra. And the face on the screen wasn't that of Patrick Blackheart. Or his son.

It was Duncan's face. At least until the camera made a jerky pan across the room to focus on the contorted features of another man. A man who had died there. A man he had killed.

A man whose name had been Paul Sorrenson.

Chapter Five

"Shut it off," Duncan demanded.

Pulling his horrified gaze away from the screen, he found Andrea's face in the darkness. The flickering light illuminated widened eyes as she watched the same images that had played out before Duncan in a thousand nightmares during the last five years.

She didn't look away, not even when his words echoed too loudly in the nearly empty room. Her lips were parted, her breathing audible, as the man who had been her husband screamed. And screamed again.

Duncan took a step toward her, drawing her eyes to him. Then, as if compelled by a force she couldn't deny, they returned to the brutal reality of how her husband had died, which was, for the first time, being revealed to her.

Duncan understood too well why she wouldn't be able *not* to watch it. Especially after last night.

The only way to prevent this was to make Helms stop the film. It was not until he had taken another step, this one bringing him closer to the computer genius, that he began to realize the more serious implication of what they were being shown.

"What the hell are you doing, Helms? Why are you showing her this?"

Even as Duncan demanded an explanation, he tried to think how this tape could have come into Helms's possession. It had been made, probably for propaganda purposes, by the terrorist cell he and Paul had been sent to eliminate on that last mission in the Middle East. After Paul's death, Duncan had been assured by Cabot that all existing copies of this atrocity had been destroyed.

As far as he was aware, the tape had never been used for its original purpose, so he had had no reason to doubt those assurances. No reason until today.

His rage overwhelming, as soon as he reached Helms, Duncan's hands fastened in the lapels of the smaller man's jacket. Despite its inherent drawbacks for handling more delicate tasks, the artificial hand was stronger now than his battered left. He dragged Helms forward, holding him almost off the floor as he shook him.

There was no reaction, other than the slide of Helms's glasses, which moved in small, jerky increments down the bridge of his nose. The gruesome sounds of what had happened five years ago in Iraq continued to reverberate through the room.

"I wouldn't do this if I were you," Helms said softly.

The quiet menace of the warning penetrated Duncan's nearly mindless rage. Then, moving slowly and deliberately, Helms turned his head, looking up and to his right.

Duncan's gaze followed to find the muzzle of an automatic rifle protruding from the window through which the images on the screen were being projected. And the red dot of its laser-targeting device, clearly visible in the darkened room, rested unwaveringly on the top of Andrea Sorrenson's head.

Duncan's eyes again found her face. Completely focused on the screen, she seemed unaware of anything else going on around her.

"Take your hands off me now," Helms ordered, his voice still soft. Still menacing.

Duncan had known all along that a threat against Andrea was the one weapon he would be incapable of fighting. A pressure he could never withstand, no matter what was at stake.

He forced his fingers to unclench, releasing the expensive silk-blend fabric they'd held. Helms staggered slightly as he was dropped. He righted himself by clutching the back of the leather chair he'd offered Duncan.

Had that offer been made so that he and Andrea would be close enough to one another to be covered by the rifle? Of course, it didn't matter that he wasn't in the direct line of fire. The red dot focused on Andrea rendered him more helpless than any other threat would have.

"How did you get that tape?" Duncan asked, his voice almost as soft as Helms.

He had become reconciled that there was no way he could keep Andrea from seeing it. The information about where Helms had obtained the tape was irrelevant, he supposed, but he wanted to know. Whether or not the bastard would tell him—

"Most things can be obtained if one offers enough money."

"And what did you *offer* for that obscenity?" Duncan asked. "And to whom?"

His gaze had gone back to the screen. The handheld camera with which the tape had been shot was focused again on Paul's face. Duncan's anguished eyes watched, just as they had then, while they tortured his partner.

And because he couldn't bear to think about what would occur only seconds from now, he turned back to Helms, his hatred so thick in his chest and throat it was difficult to breathe. It was directed at Helms, as if he were one of those who had done the unspeakable things being depicted on the screen.

"I'm sure that given your background, Culhane, you're well aware of the close ties enjoyed by the various international organizations who seek to advance a somewhat…similar agenda."

Duncan couldn't seem to concentrate on what Helms was saying. Not with the crescendoing horror of sound that accompanied the events playing out behind him. The only words out of that sentence that had any impact were "given your background."

Because Helms shouldn't be aware of his background. Not only had the External Security Team been disbanded, but all records of their activities had been expunged from the CIA's files. New identities had been created for most of them.

Duncan had been on an extended medical leave, awaiting the decision about whether or not that would become permanent, when the agency had decided to stand down the team. In the interest of national security, or so the CIA claimed, his records had also been "adjusted" so that they reflected no association with the intelligence agency.

"My background?" he repeated carefully.

"What was done was skillfully done," Helms said. "My congratulations to your employer on an *almost* flawless job. There were, however, one or two niggling irregularities. With computers it's far too easy to discover those aberrations. A detail here or there that doesn't quite match. Enough red flags that I knew you hadn't come to San Francisco because of the theft. Unless, of course, the agency was also involved in that."

"What agency?" That initial prickling of unease had become a raging torrent, but there was still too much of this he didn't understand.

"Remember that I had the luxury of a few days prior to your arrival to research Mrs. Sorrenson's claim—as well as her background. In the course of that, I discovered her husband's connections to the CIA. Then, when you showed up, and I uncovered his connections to you..."

Duncan was finally beginning to make sense of some of this. Helms had somehow discovered Paul's ties to the agency. He seemed to be under the impression the CIA had sent Andrea and then Duncan to see him for some reason other than a legitimate attempt to recover her grandmother's music box. Duncan didn't have any idea what Helms thought that might be.

"I don't know what you're talking about," he said.

Helms sounded too certain of his facts for that bluff to work. And he was undoubtedly right about the value of computers in mounting the kind of search he was talking about. Who better than Helms Enterprises to use them to do exactly what he had said?

"Let's not insult one another's intelligence, shall we? You were one of the CIA's top antiterrorist operatives, attached to a highly specialized unit known rather euphemistically as the External Security Team. And that *isn't* the kind of job you resign from, Culhane. We both know that."

This time Duncan didn't even attempt a denial. Helms was far too well-informed.

"I would be very interested in learning how the agency became aware of my activities," the millionaire went on. "I suppose it's too much to expect that you might be cooperative in providing me with that information."

The inflection at the end of the sentence rose expectantly. Obviously Helms was involved in something the CIA *would* be interested in. Duncan didn't know what that was, but it seemed unlikely at this point Helms would believe him.

"No?" Helms asked rhetorically. "Then perhaps we might be able to persuade Mrs. Sorrenson to give us that information."

The same threat that had been made by the thugs in his room last night. Helms's storm troopers? As the word formed in his brain, he realized the appropriateness of it. He had even thought of the similarity in tactics last night. Of course, the Nazis didn't have a patent on brutality for brutality's sake, but their connection to the original theft of the music box seemed to add plausibility to the idea.

As did what Helms had just said, he realized belatedly. *I'm sure that you're well aware of the close ties enjoyed by the various international organizations who seek to advance our somewhat...similar agendas.*

The terrorists who had made this tape had a well-documented animosity for the Jewish state. The very hatred that had given rise to that state had its roots in the movement which had driven Andrea's grandparents, and thousands of others like them, from Europe.

"Here's the interesting part," Helms said, turning toward the screen. A small smile lifted his thin lips. "I have to confess, I've been highly entertained by this sequence. Most ingenious. You really shouldn't miss it. No pun intended," he added, his eyes, filled with malicious enjoyment, skipping back to meet Duncan's before they returned, almost avidly, to the screen.

Duncan braced for what he knew would follow, but despite Helms's warning, he jumped when the small explosive device the terrorists had attached to his right hand went off. It was followed a fraction of a second later by the shotgun blast it had been designed to trigger.

And then there was only silence. No more screams. No sound at all, other than the soft whir of the tape.

In spite of his awareness of their present danger, Duncan closed his eyes, fighting the power of his memory of the event the others had just watched. He found himself reliving every sensation. The numbing shock followed by an incredible pain. He could smell his own flesh burning as well as the smoke from the explosive, acrid and dense in the confines of that small room.

The memories washed over him in a flood of an-

guish. To him, what had just happened was not an
image on a screen. It was something he had been
forced to live through. One of the pivotal moments
of his life. *The moment of Paul Sorrenson's death.*

Whether or not to end Paul's suffering was a decision their captors had placed in Duncan's hands.
And if Duncan found the courage to free his friend
from the horrific torture they were inflicting, the terrorists had insured that making that choice would
carry an appalling price.

It had. Not the ingenuity of the sacrifice it had demanded, which Helms had so admired. More devastating by far had been the emotional price Duncan
had paid.

The External Security Team had mounted a successful rescue less than three hours later. And despite
Griff's assurances that Paul would have died in unspeakable agony long before they arrived, Duncan
would wonder as long as he lived if he had made the
right choice.

"Duncan?"

Andrea's voice. Andrea's question. And eventually,
despite whatever Helms intended to do to them, it was
one he would have to answer.

He opened his eyes and found that the lights in the
room had been brought back up. The tape was no
longer playing.

Andrea had risen from her chair at the foot of the
long table. *The best seat in the house,* Duncan thought
bitterly, carefully chosen so that the images on the
screen would have the maximum effect.

As he met her eyes, he understood that they had.
She was leaning slightly forward. Her palms rested

on the table, supporting her weight. Her face was literally without color, eyes dark and starkly distended. And she was looking at him, rather than at the screen.

"I'm so sorry," he said.

His whisper was hoarse, and he wondered if she could possibly have understood the words.

She shook her head in response. One movement, tight and quick. Then her mouth opened. Her lips trembled, but she said nothing.

"How very touching," Helms interrupted mockingly. "You know, I confess I love the tension building at the ending, but it seems so...violent. As well as being incredibly messy. I hope you won't force us to arrange a retake of *that* particular scene, Mrs. Sorrenson."

"That—" Andrea began before the words faltered. She closed her mouth, swallowing strongly enough that the ripple of movement was visible down the length of her throat. "What happened on that tape has *nothing* to do with this."

Duncan had thought Andrea was so mesmerized by the horror playing out in front of her that she had been oblivious to Helms's explanation. Apparently she had been more aware than he had given her credit for.

"This has nothing to do with Paul or with Duncan's work for the CIA. My grandmother asked me to approach you to try to get her music box back. *That's* why I called you. That's the only reason. And then, when the box and the rest were stolen, I asked for Duncan's help to find them."

"And you made that request through a man named Griff Cabot, who, purely incidentally I suppose, happens to be a former assistant deputy director of the CIA. How stupid do you think I am, Mrs. Sorrenson? The items chosen for auction were selected solely by virtue of the fact that there was no one left to claim them. *No one.*"

"How could you possibly know that?" Andrea asked.

There was a telltale hesitation before Helms answered her. "As I've already explained to Culhane, computers are remarkably efficient instruments for making that kind of determination."

"Computer records of people from the thirties and forties? Or maybe you had a more personal assurance from people who knew for *sure* that there could be no one left to claim those objects. Exactly who are you working with, Mr. Helms?"

"Is it possible that you really *don't* know?" Helms asked, feigning incredulity. "That *would* be the ultimate theater of the absurd, wouldn't it? If you just stumbled onto this by chance."

"Stumbled onto the fact that you're selling artworks that were looted by the Nazis?" Andrea said. "That is what this is all about, isn't it?"

"Andrea," Duncan warned, having come to the unwelcome conclusion that as accurate as her assessment probably was, it wasn't the whole story. It couldn't be. Because it didn't explain, of course, how Helms had acquired the film he had just shown her or his cryptic statement about international organizations with the same agenda.

"It's all Nazi plunder, isn't it?" Andrea said, her eyes raking the array of items spread out on the table. "And you felt confident in offering it for auction because you had researched the families of the original owners and believed none of them had survived the war. I wonder how you could have been so sure of that and still been so wrong. After all, my grandmother is very much alive.''

"And what a pity that is for the two of you," Helms said. "Otherwise, you might never have become involved in this."

"I wonder how your computers missed that one," Andrea taunted. "Maybe her rescuers were more adept than we knew at hiding what they were doing. Or did my grandparents escape your computers because they changed their name. My grandfather didn't want to, but he felt he had to in order to be accepted into the medical circles in this country."

"Not such an uncommon story for the times, I'm afraid," Helms said. "A lot of people, some of them possessing very old and honorable names, were forced to change them in those days."

"Their names, but not their histories. And not their memories," Andrea said. "Those simply grew stronger through the years, despite what the Nazi apologists tried and are still trying to do to deny the reality of them."

She moved along the side of the table, the same side where Helms was standing. The laser-marker tracked her, less visible now that the lights were on, but obvious enough to hold Duncan locked in place.

"I wonder who this belonged to?" she asked, lifting the enameled piece Helms had examined earlier.

"Another Jewish bitch?" the millionaire suggested mockingly. "Now, however, it belongs to me."

"The spoils of war?"

"Spoils go to the victor," Helms said bitterly. "We weren't. At least not then."

"We?" Duncan repeated, trying to draw Helms's attention. He wasn't sure what Andrea had in mind. More importantly, he wasn't sure she was aware of the rifle.

Helms smiled. "So coy, Culhane. I do think it's a little late for that."

"Neo-Nazism," Andrea said. "All he needs is a brown shirt and one of those idiotic little mustaches."

Duncan couldn't imagine why that particular jibe would goad Helms into reaction. Or how Andrea could have known it would.

Helms started toward her, covering the distance between them in a couple of angry strides. Duncan's eyes went immediately to the projection window, from which the muzzle of the rifle protruded.

"Andrea," he yelled. "Get down!"

Instead, she raised her foot, putting the bottom of it against the side of one of the leather chairs. She shoved it toward Helms, staggering forward a little as it obediently glided away from her.

The rifle over her head fired. The bullet followed the trajectory that would take it to where Andrea had been only a split second before. Then it plowed into the table among the objects Helms had laid out there, ricocheting off the enameled vase, which overturned and rolled noisily toward the edge.

The heavy chair, sailing like a caravel over the carpet, careened toward Helms. He warded it off with his hands, using them to redirect the chair toward Duncan, who was trying to get across the room to Andrea.

He wasn't sure what he would do when he did, other than to throw his body over hers. *If* he ever reached her...

It took a second or two to push the chair out of his path. By the time he had, another shot exploded, landing in the table and sending up a spray of splinters. He flinched, reflexively turning his head to avoid them. When he turned back, Andrea was no longer there.

She also wasn't sprawled lifeless on the floor, thank God. Actually she was nowhere in sight. Duncan had time to pray that she'd had presence of mind to get under the table, before he finally reached Helms.

His back to Duncan, the millionaire was looking up, screaming at whoever was in the projection booth. Duncan's arms closed around the torso of the smaller man, pinning his elbows to his sides.

Holding a furiously squirming Helms between himself and the shooter, Duncan bent, lowering his head and trying to peer through the density of chair legs to see under the table.

He dragged his human shield with him as he retreated, still attempting to locate Andrea. On the next step back, his heel came down on the neck of the enameled vase. Off balance, his bruised left hand released, his left arm thrown out automatically to prevent his fall.

Helms took advantage of that momentary lapse, twisting away from Duncan's one-armed hold. He charged forward, still screaming at the rifleman in the projection booth.

As soon as his forward progress put some distance between them, Duncan felt a bullet tug at the cloth

of his sleeve before it struck the metal trim of the
chair he had fallen against. He heard the crack of the
rifle almost simultaneously with the sound of its ricochet.

He used the back of the chair to regain his balance,
pushing himself upright. As soon as he had, he dove
forward, arms outstretched, aiming a football-style
tackle at Helms's knees.

He managed to wrap his arms around the smaller
man's legs, bringing him down hard. He heard air
whoosh out of Helms's lungs when he hit the floor.

Duncan rolled sideways, toward the table, trying
for the slight shelter it would provide, given the angle
of fire from above and to his left. A bullet struck the
floor beside his head, forcing him to press his body
more closely against the legs of the chairs.

As he did, Helms crawled away from him, headed
toward the back of the room. Duncan started after
him, but another bullet slammed into the floor in front
of him. Pinned down by the rifle, he could do nothing
but watch Helms scramble to his hands and knees,
and then to his feet, running toward the door Duncan
suspected would lead up to the projection room.

"Duncan."

The urgency of Andrea's whisper drew his attention to the one through which they'd entered the
room. While he and Helms had been struggling, the
attention of the rifleman on them, Andrea had apparently made her way under the tables to the wall directly below the projection window. She had moved
along it, under and out of the sight of the gunman.

Now she was crouching beside the door, her right
hand lifted, its fingers poised over the dimmer control

on the wall above her head. Once she was certain he had seen her, she turned the dial, plunging the room into darkness.

Without waiting for his eyes to adjust, Duncan sprang to his feet. Keeping low, he ran across the room to where he thought the door should be. He recognized the pneumatic wheeze of the other door as it closed behind Helms, his screams echoing hollowly in the stairwell that led up to the projection room.

Finally his henchman got the message. Before Duncan could reach the outer door, gunfire exploded around him like a fireworks display.

No way, he thought, adrenaline roaring through his body, driving the muscles in his thighs like pistons. No way he could cross the room and escape that barrage unscathed. *No way.*

And then, suddenly, he was there. Falling into Andrea. Pressing her body against the door. Knowing her instantly, as he had always known he would, even in the darkness. Too aware, as bullets rained down on them—thudding into the metal of the door or bouncing noisily off it to whine away in the darkness—that the sweet, subtle scent of her body might be the last thing he would ever know.

Chapter Six

Andrea must have had her other hand on the knob. As soon as his body made contact with hers, she turned it, and together they fell through the opening door, stumbling out into the hallway.

Duncan wrapped his arms around her and jerked her roughly to the side as shots from the rifle continued to ricochet off the slowly closing door. He pushed her against the wall, sheltering her body with his.

An alarm went off, very close by, its ear-shattering noise bouncing off the concrete walls of the narrow corridor. Andrea's head came up. Her eyes met his, questioning what came next, and then, as he tried to decide, they widened.

She had turned to look over his shoulder. Below the irritating bleat of the alarm came the distinctive sound of people running along this corridor. And as the two of them listened, their breathing suspended, it became obvious that they were headed this way.

Duncan grabbed Andrea's arm, dragging her behind him as he began to run in the opposite direction. He had no idea where this hall might take them. They had been brought to the conference room from the other end. From the direction of the approaching footsteps.

The corridor seemed to go on endlessly, without any sign of an exit door or stairwell. *No way out* began to echo in Duncan's head until finally, after what felt like an eternity, they rounded a corner and came face-to-face with a bank of elevators.

He stepped forward, slapping his palm repeatedly against the up button. Their pursuers would think they'd gone down in an attempt to reach the lobby and the street. Maybe that's what they should do, Duncan had time to think, before the elevator doors opened in front of them.

The noise of pursuit was getting louder. Whether his decision was right or wrong, they couldn't hesitate.

Duncan took Andrea's arm again and pulled her inside the elevator. She leaned against the wall, the sound of their equally ragged breathing seeming to fill the car, even above the ongoing noise made by the alarm.

Duncan scanned the buttons. Incredibly, since they were in the central tower of the building, there were only three. The bottom was marked Ground. The middle one, which was unrevealingly labeled Utility, had to represent the level they were on now. And the top one had no designation at all beside it.

Almost without his volition, his index finger punched the unmarked button. Helms's penthouse office or his private apartment? Duncan wondered, as the doors began to close. Or maybe, if they were very lucky, the roof.

Of course, there was no guarantee there would be

another way down from any of those places. Other
than using these same elevators. And no guarantee,
he reminded himself, that any of the places he'd spec-
ulated about would be their destination.

Together, their eyes focused above the stainless
steel doors, they watched the floors tick off as the car
climbed. Duncan cursed himself for not at least *trying*
to bring some kind of weapon into the building.
They'd had to pass through a metal detector, so he
probably wouldn't have succeeded. The guards had
even kept their cell phones.

Those measures were routine for a company like
Helms's, which did a lot of supersensitive work for
the Department of Defense. Since the Los Alamos
fiasco, the government had demanded far more strin-
gent security from its contractors.

And he'd had no reason to question the purpose of
the call that had brought them here. No proof Helms
was involved in anything illegal, beyond the fact that
he had owned an item of somewhat questionable origins. An item he had willingly offered to give back
to its rightful owner as soon as he'd been informed
of that.

The elevator bumped to a halt, far too quickly.
They hadn't even had enough time to catch their
breath. A brief moment of safety, and no idea what
awaited them.

When the doors began to open, Duncan pushed Andrea behind him, again offering her what protection
he could. Too damned little, he acknowledged bitterly, considering the firepower of the rifle the guy in
the projection room had been using.

"Oh, my God," Andrea said.

She was so close behind him that the warmth of her breath as she whispered those words brushed his neck. Duncan's focus had been on the area just in front of the opening doors, where he had half expected to find a welcoming committee. Andrea, looking over his shoulder, was taking in the larger picture. And when Duncan lifted his eyes, he felt the same sense of stunned disbelief her voice had expressed.

The room beyond the opening doors was huge, almost cavernous in its dimness. Lining both side walls, chest high, were glass-fronted display cases. They appeared to be full of Nazi paraphernalia—helmets, uniforms, medals, documents—all carefully mounted and lit as if they were priceless works of art.

The walls above those cases had been shrouded in gold-fringed crimson banners, each centered by a swastika worked in that same gold thread. The twisted crosses, those still-familiar symbols of hate, shimmered richly in the light reflected upward from the cases.

And at the far end of the room, illuminated like some medieval shrine, was a grainy, larger-than-life photograph of the Führer. His boot heels were pressed together, his arm stretched upward, palm and fingers rigidly extended.

Directly below the picture was a raised dais, centered by a lectern. And on either side of that stage was a closed door.

As Duncan hurriedly surveyed the room, it became obvious that those doors, along with this bank of elevators, were the only ways into or out of the room. Helms wouldn't want this area to be too accessible, of course. He couldn't afford to have his employees stumble on this. Nor his clients, Duncan thought, who included not only the Department of Defense, but a myriad of other government agencies as well.

This was obviously intended only for the eyes of those who shared his perverted vision. A shrine to Nazi theology and its worshipers—past and present.

Who would be disembarking from another of these elevators at any minute, he reminded himself.

He had to mentally shake off the sense of unreality that had been created by the stunning visual impact of the room. It looked as if it had been lifted intact from 1930s Berlin.

In spite of Helms's efforts to keep this area secret and inaccessible, there would *have* to be a stairwell somewhere on this floor. Otherwise the building would never have met the fire code. Duncan didn't allow himself to think about how much Helms would be able to bribe an inspector to overlook a minor detail like that.

The fire exit must be located behind one of the two doors leading off the dais, he reasoned. The enormity of space they had to cross to reach those was daunting, but they had no other choice. These elevators made only two stops, and by now, there would be a welcoming committee at each.

"Come on," Duncan said.

Having reached that split-second decision, he again took Andrea's hand. They were nearer the right aisle, which ran between the theater-style seating and the display cases on that side.

Their footsteps echoed as they ran down it, the floor sloping slightly toward the stage. They were probably a third of the way toward their destination, when Andrea slowed, pulling against his grip.

"Guns," she said.

Without slowing, he turned his head and found her looking at the cases they were passing.

"They won't be loaded."

"Knowing Helms..." She was still resisting, so that he was almost having to drag her along.

"We *don't* know Helms," he argued, but he had slowed enough to verify she was right about the contents of the display cases.

And he understood what she meant about the millionaire. What would be the pleasure in being surrounded by all this glorious authenticity if it weren't really authentic? For someone like Helms, that *might* mean those weapons were capable of being used, just as they had been more than sixty years ago.

Might. Duncan mentally reiterated the critical part of that speculation and began to run again.

They had almost reached the dais. They couldn't afford to take the chance that there would be live ammo in those weapons or in their cases. Not even if he agreed in theory with what Andrea had suggested about the way Helms's mind worked.

Besides, the glass was probably shatterproof. Maybe even bulletproof. And they had no way—

Behind them, the bell on one of the elevators sounded. They had just run out of time. Out of chances. Out of luck.

Unless Andrea was right. Without looking back, he slowed, pulling her past him and then pushing her on toward the front.

"Head for the doors," he ordered. "There has to be a stairwell somewhere back there."

He didn't wait to see if she obeyed. Nor did he focus on what was happening back at the elevators. All he knew was that the doors of one of them would soon be opening. It would take a second or two for the eyes of its passengers to adjust to the dimness, and while they did—

He raised his right hand. The twenty thousand dollar one. The one constructed of unfeeling plastic and aluminum and polyethylene. And then, trying not to think about the damage he was about to inflict on it, he smashed the prosthesis as hard as he could against the front of the nearest display case.

As the force of the blow reverberated through the right side of his body, he realized that he hadn't even examined the contents of this particular case. When he did, his eyes frantically searching, he found, with a knee-weakening sense of relief, that it contained one of the weapons Andrea had noticed. And had he been able to choose a gun for this situation, he probably couldn't have done much better than the Schmeisser machine pistol, which rested tantalizingly on its display prongs just behind the still-intact glass.

Then, almost by accident, his eyes found the crack that snaked upward from the star marking the impact of his prosthesis. He hit that spot again and again, battering at it until the glass finally shattered.

It fell inside the case and onto the floor around his feet, the sound it made as pleasant as the elevator chime. Before the pieces had stopped falling, he had reached inside, avoiding the remaining shards that clung to the frame.

He instructed his fingers to grasp the stock of the Schmeisser. The grip of his artificial hand, which had been delicate enough to grasp a paper brochure and take it from Andrea's, wouldn't obey. It refused to close around the gun.

Almost before he had had time to comprehend that, a bullet slammed into the broken glass beside his head. It exploded into a million pieces, splinters stinging his cheek as they flew outward.

Definitely not bullet proof.

He ducked, swinging his body to the right, crouching down between the case he'd broken into and the next in line. He lowered his head as the fronts of several others cases along the wall shattered in the frenzy of firing.

They might be aiming at him, he realized, but the bullets were striking above his head. Above the tops of the theater seats, which were offering him some protection.

As he knelt between the cases, his eyes rose to the dais below the Führer's picture. There was no sign of Andrea. Both doors were still closed. He could only hope she'd reached safety behind one of them before the shooting had begun.

So far their pursuers were being cautious. Maybe they knew about the arsenal in these cases. If that *was* the reason for their caution, then it might argue that Andrea was right.

Or maybe they believed he'd smuggled his own weapon past the detection devices. Whatever was causing them to be careful now, they wouldn't continue to be if he didn't return their fire.

He glanced up, locating the machine pistol, to the

left and above his head. As the firing from the elevator began to diminish, he reached for it again, this time using his left hand. A spray of bullets from an automatic weapon cut a swath across the case before he could grab the gun and bring it down.

He ducked once more, while glass rained down on his head and shoulders. As soon as it stopped, he looked up again, examining the gun. It didn't appear to have been damaged, but the "ifs" in this situation were compounding.

What if the gun wasn't loaded? What if the firing mechanism had been damaged by one of those bullets? What if—

Before his brain could compose the next question, a burst of music roared out, echoing thunderously throughout the room. He glanced up, trying to find its source.

The speakers it came from had been cunningly concealed behind the red silk flags. Their size and power was painfully obvious, as the song, a thousand voices strong, swelled.

Deutschland, Deutschland, über alles. The words of the Nazi anthem reverberated from the high ceiling and bounced eerily off the concrete walls. Almost too loud to allow him to think. And if *he* couldn't think—

He strained upward, the bruised and swollen fingers of his left hand stretched toward the gun. Again, they were driven away by a frenzied burst of firing.

Whoever was in the elevator had adjusted more quickly to the shock of the music than he. Of course, they had probably heard it all before.

As soon as the firing became sporadic, Duncan raised his head, peering through the dimness toward the back of the room and the bank of elevators. Three or four figures were moving cautiously out of the open car, their guns in firing position. If they met no resistance, the rest of them—however many there were—would soon come pouring out as well.

Suddenly, in addition to the roar of the music, images began to appear and then fade on the screen at the front of the room. The picture of the Führer morphed into one of marching Nazi troops, goose stepping out of history, and then into planes dropping bombs on some city below, each image visible long enough to give the viewer time to identify it before it was replaced with another.

Helms's technological wizardry combined with Goebbels' unfailing sense of showmanship, Duncan thought as he watched. And with the Nazi anthem booming in the background, it was damned impressive. And damned distracting.

The shifts in light and darkness reflected from the changing images on the screen created shadows in the auditorium, fooling the eye and the brain. As soon as he realized that, Duncan took advantage of it, his body surging recklessly upward again. This time, his left hand closed around the Schmeisser, ripping it from the prongs.

He turned, his index finger settling over the trigger as his heart composed the prayer his mind didn't dare to frame. It was quickly answered as the decades-old machine gun sprayed destruction across the open elevator doors.

Two of the exposed figures went down in the first barrage. The others ducked back inside, but Duncan didn't stop firing. All the steel that surrounded them would be his ally.

As he continued to shoot, 9 mm bullets ricocheted off the metal, their whine adding to the din from the hidden amplifiers. Someone cried out, and because he wasn't sure where Andrea had taken refuge, his finger eased on the trigger as he tried to listen.

The music beat against his eardrums, drowning other noises. He began to back toward the dais, aiming short bursts at the elevators, just to keep whoever was still alive in them contained.

He expected the arrival of reinforcements at any moment, surprised that they hadn't already shown up. Of course, Helms couldn't send regular security up here, and it was always possible there had been only a handful of his trusted neo-Nazi henchmen in the building.

If so, he and Andrea had gotten lucky. If he could hold the present contingent in place until he reached the doors behind the stage—

As he began to back up the stairs leading to the dais, someone got brave enough to poke his head out of the elevator. Another burst from the Schmeisser drove him back. By that time Duncan was halfway across the stage, running backward.

"Duncan."

He turned his head in response. Andrea was huddled behind the lectern. In the second he allowed himself to examine her before his gaze flicked back to the elevators, he had reassured himself that she wasn't hurt.

"There's a control panel for everything in the room in here," she said.

An access door on the back of the lectern was open. Inside he could see a board full of dials and switches and buttons. Andrea had apparently been experimenting with them, which explained the origin of the music and projections.

"Leave it," he ordered. He couldn't see how Helms's toys could help them any more.

"Wait," she said, turning away from the control board to look up at the screen. The intermittent patterns of light and dark reflected downward from the changing images made her skin appear very pale. "It's coming up again."

Something on the screen she wanted him to see, Duncan realized. Something she thought was important enough to delay them. His eyes made another sweep of the back of the room.

Apparently he'd made believers of whoever was left in the elevator. No one seemed eager to make another excursion out. He wasn't sanguine enough to believe they were all dead. Not yet.

"Now," Andrea said.

Obediently he turned and raised his eyes. On the screen was a far more modern image than the few he had watched from down in the auditorium. This one, too, was instantly recognizable. It had been shown over and over again on millions of TVs across the nation last spring.

The blasted shell of what had once been the FBI regional office in Parkhurst, Wyoming, towered above their heads. There were none of the familiar pictures of the victims of that bombing to accompany it. The next image up was a map of the continental United States.

Although the Parkhurst bombing, which had been laid at the door of a radical local militia group, had been caused by TNT, on the projected map a small, mushroom-shaped cloud appeared over its approximate location. It blossomed upward in an eye-catching animation. And then, as it dissipated, other markings began to appear across the map.

Starting in the Northeast, red bull's eye-shaped targets sprang up, each neatly labeled. Their appearances marched across the states faster than he could identify them. Temple Emanu-El in New York. The National Holocaust Museum in D.C. The Southern Poverty Law Center in Montgomery.

As Duncan tried to concentrate on the names, behind him the chime that indicated the arrival of another elevator sounded. He and Andrea turned from the map simultaneously, their eyes meeting.

He tilted his head toward the door in a silent command. Without further argument Andrea leaped to her feet and started across the stage toward the door on the right. Duncan followed, backing, the muzzle of the machine pistol still pointed toward the elevators.

Only now did he think about the possibility that the door would be locked. He turned his head in time to see the knob turn under Andrea's fingers. Then, eyes focused once more on the elevators, he took a couple of giant steps backward, pushing Andrea into the darkness of the room behind that door.

Using his right elbow, he closed it, hoping the music would hide the noise it had made as it shut. Holding the Schmeisser between his elbow and his side, he reached out with his left hand, feeling for an inside lock he could turn against the invaders. There wasn't one.

Fighting the urge to slam his fist into the door in frustration, he leaned against it instead, putting his ear on the wood. Maybe he could tell what was going on out there by sound. The music was too loud, however. The door literally vibrated in its frame with each throb of the bass.

''There's a window,'' Andrea said.

She had been surveying their surroundings while he'd been trying to discover what was happening outside. Duncan straightened, looking over his shoulder.

The square of light was visible through the thick material of the draperies that had been drawn across it. As he assessed its size, he pictured in his mind the central tower of Helms's headquarters. He couldn't imagine what possible use that window could be to them, considering how high they were.

There had to be another way out. It didn't make sense that this area would be self-contained.

Andrea had felt her way across the room to pull aside the drape. As sunlight flooded in, the room's purpose became depressingly obvious. The walls were lined, floor to ceiling, with shelves, all of which were filled with items probably used during events held in the auditorium.

There were stacks of video and audio cassettes, as well as a virtual library of pamphlets. Everything was labeled with stickers attached to the edge of the shelves they rested on. There were also Nazi uniforms, remarkably authentic looking, also neatly marked by size.

A couple of cardboard boxes had the word Banners

written on them in black marker. Flags for the dais? Or more of the silk hangings they'd seen in the auditorium? Whatever they contained, it was obvious that all of this, like the memorabilia in the display cases, would have to be hidden from outsiders in order for Helms to maintain his charade of normality.

"There has to be another way out of here," Andrea said, echoing his thinking of a few seconds ago.

He wasn't sure anymore that there would be. Maybe the stairwell he'd been counting on was on the opposite side of the stage. If this room were simply a storeroom for props, there wouldn't be another exit from it.

His gaze searched the perimeters. There were four chairs, stacked one on top of the other in the far corner. They weren't folding chairs, and their metal legs looked fairly substantial.

He crossed the room in a few quick strides, planning to wedge the tall back of one of them under the knob of the door. A simple, but effective method of keeping someone from opening a door inward. Even if it didn't keep Helms's henchmen out for long, it would at least give them some warning they'd arrived.

He had no illusions that Helms would allow them to leave this building alive. From the time the millionaire had rolled the tape of Paul's death, that had been a foregone conclusion. He would never have exposed his beliefs to the two of them otherwise. From the moment he'd learned of their association with the CIA, Helms had intended to kill them.

All they had done so far was to slow down his plan. And in the course of doing that, they had learned more about Helms's terrifying objectives. Unless Duncan could devise some way to get them out of this room, however...

He juggled the Schmeisser under his arm as he tried to disentangle the top chair from the others. Finally he laid the gun on its seat and used his left hand to lift the chair away from the stack far enough that he could get the useless right one under it. He carried the chair over to the door and then tilted it, wedging the back under the knob.

He picked up the machine pistol again and turned to find Andrea setting another of the chairs under the window. As he watched, she climbed onto the seat. She began running her fingers around the edge of the window, obviously searching for the mechanism that would allow her to open it.

He knew what she was thinking. She and Paul had done a lot of weekend rock climbing. She knew the techniques involved in rappelling, and she had probably done a bit of it, but rappelling down a rock face was a world away from something like this. It was a damn long way to the ground from up here.

"It probably wasn't designed to open," he warned. "Not this high up."

As if to dispute his opinion, there was a soft whir as one side of the window slid behind the other. The opening created was narrow, maybe eighteen inches across, but it was definitely an opening.

Andrea turned, grinning at him almost triumphantly. His chest tightened with a surge of love and admiration. She knew the odds against them as well as he did, but she was still fighting, still looking for a way out. Refusing to give up.

"There's a balcony," she reported, turning back to the window. "It's not large, but…I think you could stand on it."

"Fire escape?"

"Nothing like that. Not that I can see. But all we need to do is one floor."

"*One* floor?"

She turned her head, meeting his eyes. "A floor with normal elevators. Phones. Maybe even people. There has to be *somebody* in this place who isn't involved in this insanity."

There would be. Probably a very small percentage of Helms's employees were aware of his philosophy. He couldn't have managed to keep his involvement in the neo-Nazi movement a secret otherwise.

The problem wasn't that there wouldn't be someone willing to help them. The problem was, once they got out that window, how in the hell they were going to get back into the building.

There had to be some other way. Some way besides the near-suicidal feat of trying to climb down the wall of a twenty-story building. At one time, he might have been willing to try that, given that they were trapped. Now, however…

The silence built as Andrea waited for his answer. And then something bumped against the door. He turned, his eyes focusing on the knob. As he watched, it began to turn. The door opened a crack before the legs of the chair under its knob caught.

And held. And finally Duncan remembered to breath. Just as he did, someone hit the outside of the door with enough force to cause it to shudder. The legs of the chair dug more deeply into the floor as pressure was applied from the outside.

Whoever was out there would eventually find something heavy enough to batter the door with so that, if the chair didn't give, the wood itself would. Or, more frightening, they might realize that they didn't have to be inside this room to use those automatic weapons.

Duncan backed toward Andrea and the window, his eyes locked on the door that shook with each repeated blow. As he passed the shelves he'd scanned before, he reached out with his damaged right hand, using it the only way he could now—like a club—to sweep one of the boxes marked Banners onto the floor. The lid separated from the carton as it struck, releasing a flood of red silk.

"Tie them together," he whispered, "end to end."

Andrea's eyes widened in comprehension. Then she scrambled down from her perch before the window to obey.

Chapter Seven

Duncan watched the door, the muzzle of the gun he'd taken from the display case pointed at it, as she tied the ends of those long red banners together. Adding urgency to her trembling fingers, the attempts of Helms's men to batter their way in had become increasingly frantic. She wasn't sure which would give out first, the door or their patience.

She pulled the ends of another knot tight and glanced up. Not at the door, but at the man she had drawn into this. *A favor for an old friend.* That's all it was supposed to have been. Her motives hadn't been that pure, of course. If not for what had happened between them last night, he would never have known that.

Duncan turned to check on her progress. Kneeling beside the carton, she had already tied together all the strips that were within her reach. When he realized that, he bent, trying to scoop up a piece of silk that hadn't tumbled out of the box.

It was only then, seeing how awkwardly he handled the fabric, that she realized why he wasn't helping her. Not, as she'd originally believed, because he needed to hold the weapon on the door.

"What's wrong with your hand?" she demanded, leaning forward to retrieve the piece of silk that eluded him.

His lips flattened, but he didn't answer before he turned again to the door. One of the hinges had begun to tear away from the frame, the wood splintering under the repeated blows.

"Duncan?"

Still no answer. She looked up at the frame, knowing it would only be a minute or two before the top of the door would give under the assault.

"You aren't going to do this, are you?"

Her voice was almost accusing. He had never intended to go out that window. This was all a trick to get *her* out, while he stayed behind and tried to hold off that rich bastard's imbecilic followers.

She had no doubt she could rappel down to the next level. Duncan believed she could, too, or he would never have suggested this. *She* wasn't the problem. Neither was having someone guard the door.

She had just seen the problem, and her stomach tightened with anxiety and concern. If he thought she was going to leave him behind—

"I'm not going without you," she said flatly. "If that's what you're thinking, then you can just think again."

It was a phrase her mother had used when she was a little girl. And it sounded childish in this situation.

At least it made him turn to look at her again. The light from the window behind her illuminated the lean planes and angles of his face. So beautifully and completely masculine, at least to her. But then, they always had been.

Suddenly the blue eyes lightened. It took a second or two for her to recognize that what she was seeing was amusement. And then, the movement very slight, his lips tilted. That same subtle motion she had classified yesterday as *almost* a smile.

Had that urbane, civilized lunch been only yesterday? It seemed as if they had spent a lifetime fleeing from Helms and his goons. And then, despite the danger, she acknowledged that however long they had been in this together, it hadn't been nearly long enough.

"I guess if *you* believed we were going out that window," Duncan said, "we can hope they will."

"We aren't." It wasn't a question.

"Not yet, at any rate."

"But…we want them to think we have," she said, working her way through what he intended.

As she pronounced the last word the door reverberated, the screws that had been holding the top hinge in place finally giving way and pulling free of the broken wood. *One down and two to go.*

"So what *are* we going to do?" she asked, still whispering.

"Play hide-and-seek," Duncan said. "Give me that." He held out his hand for the string of silk banners she had tied together.

His right hand, she realized. The one he had never allowed to touch her. The one he had sacrificed to put a merciful end to Paul's agony. *With my own hand.*

He hadn't lied to her about his role in her husband's death, but he had made no attempt to explain or excuse what he'd done. Just as she hadn't tried to explain to him why she had married his best friend.

"About Paul…" she began.

"There isn't time for that," he objected harshly.

"There's time for this."

As she said it, she placed her fingers on top of the prosthesis. She didn't know what she'd expected. Not the warmth of flesh and bone, obviously. Maybe something slick and hard and cold. It wasn't, but because of what was suddenly in his eyes, she was almost unaware of the feel of the artificial hand beneath her fingers.

"Thank you," she said. "I know Paul would want me to tell you that. What you did—" Her voice broke unexpectedly, and her eyes filled with tears, but once more she denied them. "That was the act of a friend. An enormously courageous friend."

His lips flattened again as he swallowed, but he didn't look away. And he didn't remove his fingers from under hers.

Neither of them moved, eyes holding, until another blow hammered the door. The sound of wood splintering was too clear, even above the throb of the music outside. *Deutschland, Deutschland, über alles.*

She closed her eyes. Maybe to hide what she knew would be in them. Maybe to control the threatening tears. Maybe simply to breathe a prayer that whatever he was planning would work.

They had had so little time. And she wondered why it had taken her so long to find the courage to call Griff.

"Andy?" he said.

She opened her eyes to smile at him. That was what

Paul had always called her, but she had not forgotten it had been Duncan who had first shortened her name to that masculine diminutive.

She lifted her hand from his, and reaching into her lap, laid the banners she'd tied together over his wrist. In exchange, he handed her the machine pistol.

"If they start to come through the door, just squeeze the trigger and keep squeezing until it's empty."

Paul's voice echoed those same instructions in her head. She got to her feet as Duncan moved toward the window. Only then did she turn her attention, and the gun, toward the broken door.

Even above the noise outside, she heard when he pulled the drape back across the window, darkening the room. Not all the way across, but enough to shut out most of the light.

She heard Duncan's footsteps approaching behind her, but she kept her eyes fastened on the shivering door. He put his left hand under her elbow to guide her across the dark room. The tiny sliver of light from the window lay in a narrow ribbon across the floor.

Duncan positioned her against the wall on the side of the door where the knob was located. The wood of the frame would give before the metal legs of the chair collapsed, which meant that Helms's men would come in through the other side, where the hinges were. They would shove the door inward—

And Duncan thought the two of them could somehow hide behind it? At the realization of what his plan was, fear settled in her stomach, making her nauseated.

This wouldn't work. It *couldn't* work. There wasn't

enough room. Helms's bastards would push open the door, and then they'd see them. Someone would turn on the lights. Search the room. Something...

She expressed none of those doubts. Instead, she crouched beside him, her body pressed as close to the wall as she could get it. Duncan had determined that this was their best chance. He was the one with all the experience. If he thought this would work—

It all happened at once, almost too quickly for her fear to grow. And yet somehow, despite the speed, it seemed to unfold as if she were watching a film running in slow motion.

Helms's men kicked at the bottom of the door, and the last of the hinges pulled away from the frame, the sound like paper tearing. Because it wasn't hinged on the other side—the side where they were hidden—the door didn't open. The men outside powered the crack wide enough for one of them to squeeze his upper body inside. They watched as he reached around the broken door, his hand groping toward the chair Duncan had shoved under the knob.

The muscles in Duncan's left arm, which she was leaning against, tensed in anticipation. If this didn't work, he would try to shoot it out with them. And she had no idea how much ammunition he had left.

"Son of a bitch," the one who'd been trying to come through the door said. "They went out the frigging window."

A couple of others crowded into the opening to verify what he had just said. Andrea pulled her eyes from the doorway, knowing she could do nothing to influence what was going to happen. She focused on what the men in the doorway were seeing—a thin shaft of light leading the eye to that window.

The chair she had put under it had been laid sideways on the high sill, visible only in silhouette because it was now lying in front of the drapes. Somehow Duncan had managed, probably by using his teeth, to loop one end of that string of red silk banners around the metal framework of the chair, tying it between the seat and the high back. The rest of the fabric had been draped over the side of the chair and allowed to hang out the open window, where the silk trembled in the breeze.

The shaft of sunlight fell directly on that blaze of color. Duncan had even made it appear that the slight opening left in the curtain had been an accident.

And the ruse worked. It was a little frightening that it worked so well.

Almost in disbelief that it was going to be this simple, Andrea listened as the men who been battering at the door abandoned it, running back across the wooden stage. As the sound of their footsteps disappeared under the Sturm und Drang of the music, she waited until she felt Duncan move.

He eased up soundlessly until he was standing, the machine gun still pointing at the door. Her eyes followed his rise, but he motioned her to remain where she was with a quick downward movement of his right forearm. He took a step and then another, moving away from the wall and avoiding the finger of light coming in from the window.

And then he paused. It was obvious by his posture that he was listening. Heart lodged in her throat, she listened as well, trying to hear anything over the music. Wishing she could take back the flick of the switch responsible for that ungodly din.

Duncan ducked across the light, positioning himself behind the door that tilted drunkenly, held upright only by the chair under its knob. He leaned forward to peer through the opening Helms's men had forced on the hinged side, and again she held her breath.

Finally he motioned her forward. She stood, hurrying across the light to place herself at his back. She resisted the urge to put her arms around his waist and rest her cheek against his shoulder. To enjoy, even briefly, the sense of security that would give.

In a few seconds they would have to go through that door. Only then would they know if their trick had really fooled anyone.

Duncan eased through the crack. She expected gunfire. A command for him to step forward with his hands up. Anticlimactically, there was nothing. For a long time there was no sound but the music and the pounding of her heart.

"Come on."

Duncan's voice. She slipped through the opening, eager to be with him again and not alone, no matter what came next. When she emerged, he was standing a few feet beyond the broken door, his gaze sweeping the auditorium.

Without looking at her, he tilted his head toward the door on the other side of the stage. She had believed that's where Helms's men had gone. It was possible, of course, that the music had distorted the sound of those running footsteps enough to mislead her about their direction.

As she hesitated, Duncan turned his head, glancing

at her over his shoulder. His eyes met hers, questioning, before they returned to their surveillance.

Experience, she reminded herself. *Not instinct.*

She ran toward the second door, her body
crouched, as she tried to make as little noise as possible. The volume of the anthem made that precaution
ludicrous.

As she passed the lectern, she wanted to reach over
and turn the damn thing off, but she knew that would
be a dead giveaway that they were still up here. *If*
there were anyone near enough to be aware of the
blessed silence.

When she reached the opposite door, she opened it
to reveal a corridor, dimly lit by skylights. Far more
promising than her original choice. She held the door
as Duncan backed through.

As soon as he had, he turned, redirecting the muzzle of the machine gun. He led the way down the
hall, running past what appeared to be offices. Clearly
visible at the end was another doorway and an Exit
sign.

All they needed was to get down one floor. To
phones. To normal people working at normal jobs.

As they approached the end of the hallway, however, Duncan slowed. "Damn it to hell," he said under his breath.

Her eyes found what he'd already seen. Emergency
Exit Only. Which meant—

"Alarms," she said aloud.

"Maybe they go off at the fire department. Or
maybe we'll get lucky and get security up here."

"Duncan—"

"We've got no choice," he said sharply before he

reached out with his left hand, again holding the weapon with his elbow, and turned the knob.

Nothing happened. Nothing except Duncan bounding down the stairs as if something had. Running as if they were still being pursued. Startled by the lack of caution with which he was taking the stairs, she followed, one hand on the railing as her feet clattered down the concrete steps.

She had been expecting Duncan to stop at the next landing, but he kept going, long legs seeming to eat up the distance. Two, three, four, five floors. Her chest had begun to ache before he skidded to a stop and peered through the glass portion at the top of one of the doors. Apparently satisfied by what he saw, he reached out to turn the knob. It didn't move.

"Bastard," he said succinctly, the word almost devoid of emotion. And then he began to run down the next flight.

"What if they're all locked?" she called, trailing him.

"Then eventually we'll discover where this comes out."

At the next two doors, he stopped, and, holding the machine pistol between his arm and his side, tried the knobs. The second time he did, she moved past him, leading the way down the next flight of steps.

When she came to the landing, she reached out and tried the door almost without slowing down. After the others, she expected it to be locked. She wasn't disappointed.

She repeated the action at each floor as they continued to descend. Eventually she lost count of them. Enough that she knew they must be near ground level.

And then, as she was halfway down the next set of the stairs, the door on the landing below them opened.

The routine of trying the knob and then moving on had become automatic, so that she was caught off guard. The man who opened the door seemed almost as shocked, his pupils dilating and his mouth gaping as he stared up at the two of them.

Building security or one of Helms's goons? How the hell could they know?

Even as the question formed, she knew. No uniform. Shaved head. Young. And the pistol he held in his hand, raising its muzzle to point at her chest.

Despite the fact that she had been running on autopilot, Duncan had never relaxed his vigilance. Before the man had time to pull the trigger, he cut him down with a burst from the machine pistol, its stutter so close she flinched, putting her hands over her ears.

Duncan leaped past her, pushing the dying man out of his way and grabbing at the knob of the closing door with his right hand. The fingers of the prosthesis wouldn't close around it. By the time he'd juggled his weapon to get his left into play, the door had slammed shut.

"Son of a bitch," he hissed in frustration. And with the next breath, he flattened himself against the wall behind the door, motioning her to do the same.

The man who opened the door this time had been warned by the shots. More cautious, he led with his weapon. Duncan shot it out of his hand and then fired a burst into his chest. The man toppled forward onto the landing, but his legs prevented the door from closing.

Duncan stepped over him, putting his shoulder

against the inside of the door. He waited a few seconds and then moved into the hall. Andrea followed, stepping over the man Duncan had killed without even looking down.

The hall appeared to be deserted, fluorescent lights gleaming softly off the polished floor. This time they didn't have to make a decision. There was only one way to go.

As soon as she had cleared the door, Duncan headed in that direction at a run. Andrea followed, hoping he had a better idea of the layout of this place than she did.

There was a sound behind her. Still running, she looked back to see Helms and a couple of skinheads come out of the door she and Duncan had used to escape the stairwell.

"Duncan," she shouted.

"Please don't make me kill you, Mrs. Sorrenson," Helms said.

The warning seemed almost farcical. After all, he had been trying to kill them all along.

Ahead of her, Duncan had stopped, turning in response to her call. When he saw Helms and the others, he brought the machine gun into firing position.

The footsteps behind her were too close, although she was running as fast as she could. At least she had been until Duncan whirled, pointing the gun in her direction.

"Andy, get down."

Before she could obey, a pair of arms wrapped around her chest, jerking her upward so violently that her feet left the floor. She kicked back and had the satisfaction of feeling her heel connect solidly with the guy's shin. He grunted a profanity, but his hold tightened rather than loosened, locking her arms to her sides.

She twisted and turned, but he continued to half drag, half carry her backward, keeping her body between him and Duncan. And she knew with a surety that both infuriated and touched her that Duncan would never pull that trigger as long as she was in the way.

"Put down the Schmeisser, Culhane. It's over, and you've lost," Helms said.

Frantically Andrea increased her efforts to break free of the man who held her, twisting, turning and kicking, but nothing seemed to have any effect.

"Shoot him," she yelled.

If Duncan surrendered, they were both dead.

"How clever, Mrs. Sorrenson. And how noble. I warned you we might have to stage a reenactment of the incident in Iraq. The stakes are somewhat higher this time, and far more interesting. Did you know that the guards at the camps sometimes gave people this same kind of choice?"

"You Nazi bastard," Andrea said.

Given what they now knew about Helms's plans, the stakes were much higher. If Duncan were willing to shoot her, then he could kill Helms. And if he weren't, Helms would carry out that campaign of terror they had seen outlined on the map upstairs.

"There's something extraordinary about moral dilemmas," the millionaire went on, his voice musing. "And I find it amazing there are still those who would choose nobility over survival. I'm afraid I find it difficult to empathize with their foolishness, however."

"Shoot him," Andrea said again, trying to imbue the command with every ounce of influence she might have over Duncan Culhane.

She knew now that she had a great deal. He had confessed as much last night. *That isn't the way I've always imagined this. Not the way I wanted it to be.*

Duncan loved her. Maybe he hadn't told her that in so many words, but she knew he did.

"What shall it be, Culhane?" Helms challenged. "You can't shoot us without hitting Mrs. Sorrenson. Not with that particular weapon and at this range."

"You can't even think about letting him get away, Duncan," Andrea argued. "No one else knows what he is or what he's planning. You have to stop him. Shoot the bastard, damn it."

"Stalemate," Helms taunted. "Or should that be checkmate." And then, in an entirely different tone, "Kill him."

The other man, who had been standing by Helms, also sheltered behind Andrea's body, began to move. He would have to, she realized, in order to have a clear shot.

A shot at Duncan, who wouldn't shoot back. Not with her in the way.

She bent her knees, lifting her feet off the ground to become a dead weight. She had caught the man who had wrapped his arms around her unprepared, watching the drama that was playing out before him. As he tried to secure his grip, she let her feet drop to the ground, pushing off to the left with all her strength—right into the path of the man Helms had just ordered to shoot Duncan.

Thrown off balance by her lunge, the man who held

her staggered sideways, bumping into the other one just as his gun went off. At the same time, Andrea gave another adrenaline-driven twist to her upper body, breaking apart the locked hands of the man who had grabbed her from behind.

Momentum carried her to the side. She began to fall, changing the motion to a roll. Before she hit the floor, she heard the now-familiar chatter of the machine pistol. She closed her eyes and put her hand up as blood splattered over her from the two men Duncan had just cut down.

And Helms? She opened her eyes to find Duncan standing calmly in the center of the corridor, the Schmeisser held professionally in his left hand. Automatically she turned to look for the millionaire.

He had flattened himself against the opposite wall. *Shoot him.* Her mouth was too dry to scream the command, but she sent it telepathically as Helms began to draw a pistol from his inside coat pocket. *Shoot him.*

When he didn't, her eyes again found Duncan, watching as his finger squeezed the trigger. And this time, instead of the reassuring clatter of the machine pistol, there was only a hollow click. The sound seemed to echo along the corridor more loudly than the gunfire had.

With a wordless roar, Duncan threw the pistol at Helms and began to run toward him. *Too far. Too far.*

The words beat at her brain as once again everything slowed. Duncan's legs, which had seemed to fly down the stairs, were moving now as if through water. Or a dream. *Too slow. Too far.*

And then, as she began to turn again toward Helms

to try to judge if Duncan could possibly reach him before he could get the gun out, her eyes brushed over the weapon the skinhead had dropped as he died.

It was lying at her feet. *Too far. Too slow.*

Refusing to accept that, she threw herself forward, grabbing the pistol with both hands, her finger fumbling to find the trigger. Two shots seemed to explode as one, the second merely an echo of the first.

Her eyes locked on her target, gradually she began to realize that hers had been the first. Helms's hand clutched spasmodically at the center of his chest, as his eyes focused with stunned disbelief on her face.

Jewish bitch echoed. And she heard it this time with a sense of satisfaction.

Then Helms fell back against the wall, seeming to melt down it as his knees gave way. The pistol he'd aimed at Duncan fell from fingers suddenly gone lax. It struck the floor and skittered away.

He continued to slide, almost as if he were sitting down. She might even have believed that if it weren't for the smear of red on the wall behind him.

He landed with a small bump, hard enough that his glasses slid down that thin, freckled nose. By then, the eyes behind them were blank and lifeless.

"For my family," she said. "For *all* of them, you bastard."

And finally, the tears that had threatened upstairs overwhelmed her control. She was sobbing openly by the time Duncan reached her. It didn't seem to matter.

Nothing mattered but that he was holding her. And this time it felt as if he never intended to let her go.

Chapter Eight

"Griff sends his apologies."

She looked up from the drink he'd fixed for her before he had called Cabot. Standing in the doorway to her kitchen, Duncan looked as exhausted as she felt.

"His apologies for not knowing what Helms was up to?" she asked. "I don't see how he could have figured that out in the time frame he had to work in."

"I think he feels responsible."

"I feel responsible," she said.

A crease formed between his brows, and then he stepped into the room, walking over to the island where she was sitting. In the exact spot where he had sat last night, several light years ago.

"You understand I'm not sorry Helms is dead instead of me," he said. "I *am* sorry you were the one who had to kill him."

He thought she was remorseful over Helms's death, she realized. And nothing could be further from the truth.

"How many men have you killed, Duncan?" she asked. Only when she saw the impact of that unthinking question in his face did she realize what she had done.

"Enough," he said, his voice unchanged despite that flicker of emotion.

"I didn't mean Paul," she said quickly.

"I know."

"I've never killed anyone. I never even thought about the possibility that I might. But…it took me weeks to get the images of the Parkhurst bombing out of my head. Helms would have financed that kind of thing again and again if we hadn't stopped him. You're probably the only person in the world I will ever say this to, but deep down inside I'm glad I was the one who pulled that trigger. It seemed like a kind of justice. I keep thinking about everything my grandparents suffered. And for someone like Helms…"

The words trailed. She didn't need to finish that thought. Duncan understood every aspect of what she was thinking.

He and the other members of Griff's team knew better than anyone why someone like Helms had to be stopped—by any necessary means. After all, they had devoted their lives to doing exactly that. They still were.

It had taken its toll. Duncan's eyes were shadowed with fatigue, the thin skin around them discolored like old bruises. Too little sleep. Too much stress. Pain and exhaustion. A ruined hand. *Those* were the things she felt responsible for.

"When I said I was responsible, I meant for getting you into this," she said.

"You'd rather have handled it alone?"

There was a trace of amusement in the question.

And it was reflected in those tired eyes. Just as it had been when she'd thought they were going to climb out that window and rappel down the side of a twenty-story office tower.

She would have, too. She couldn't see any other way out, and if Duncan had told her that's what they had to do, she would have followed him. Anywhere.

To hell and back. *Just as Paul had.*

Except Paul hadn't come back. And they had. They were, remarkably, still alive. With another chance to get this right. Maybe their last chance.

"I didn't want to do it alone," she said. "But asking for your help…I guess I should tell you now that the choice Griff made wasn't exactly random."

The crease reappeared. "I don't understand."

"It wasn't because you were here. In San Francisco. I asked Griff about you. I called him about the theft, but in the course of that conversation—"

She took a breath, knowing that she was probably betraying Cabot's trust. But knowing also that she needed to be honest about this. She had wasted enough time. They both had. If she needed any further lesson about the fragility of life, she had gotten it today.

"I asked for you specifically. I asked him to assign you to help me," she finished. His eyes didn't change. "You'd already figured that out," she guessed.

"Part of it. I wasn't sure why."

"Because I wanted to see you again. I needed to tell you—"

When the silence after that broken phrase became tense, he filled it.

"To tell me what?"

"I want another chance. That I want us to have another chance," she amended.

"Andy…"

"I know you think there's too much between us. Too much baggage we'd have to get past."

"You can't make it go away. Neither can I."

"Paul's death? But I know the truth about that now. Maybe I should even be grateful to Helms for that. Would you have ever told me?"

He shook his head, the motion tight, his eyes still on her face.

"I've told you how I feel about what you did," she went on. "Paul would have been grateful. Just as I am."

"If I'd waited, he might still have been alive when the rescue party broke through."

"Griff said you were lucky to be alive," she said. Involuntarily her gaze fell to the hand he'd lost that day. "You couldn't have kept Paul alive. If you hadn't done exactly what you did—"

He shook his head once, the sharp movement cutting off her words.

"Maybe if it hadn't happened that way," he said. "If Paul had been killed in any other way…." He took a breath instead of finishing.

The sum total of their relationship. Maybe.

She couldn't push this any more. Not tonight. They were both exhausted. Maybe after they'd had some sleep. Maybe.

"Griff asked me to stay with you until he can get someone else out here to track down the items that were stolen. That should be tomorrow afternoon at the latest, if everything goes according to plan."

Giving Cabot's efficiency, it would.

"Of course," she said. She couldn't force Duncan to give this a chance. Maybe in time. *Maybe.*

He had already started toward the door, when he turned.

"I couldn't have asked for a better partner today."

"Not bad for an amateur," she said. Her smile was slightly tremulous, surely forgivable in the circumstances.

"Not bad for *anybody*. And I worked with the best."

"I know," she said, thinking about the good man who had been her husband. "Thank you for saying that."

He nodded again, and then he turned toward the door. This time he didn't look back.

THE WATER BEAT AGAINST the back of his neck, easing the tightness along his spine. It had been a hell of a couple of days, he acknowledged.

Dealing with Helms and his goons had almost been the least of it. He had a lot of experience with that kind of thing. Dealing with Andrea, however…

He turned, raising his chin to let the water cascade against his chest. Trying not to think about what she'd said. Trying not to think about how damned fragile she'd looked tonight. Trying not to think about her at all.

He reached for the soap. He could only prolong this so long. Eventually the hot water would run out. And hiding here wouldn't solve anything.

Griff had promised he'd get someone out to relieve him tomorrow. Less than twenty-four hours and this would be over. He could go home to New York. Lose himself again in the work Phoenix was doing. Fulfilling a need which seemed never-ending.

He found satisfaction in that. He was accomplishing the things he had always wanted with his life. Important things.

When Andrea had married Paul, he'd had to become accustomed to the idea that she was never going to be his. He would become accustomed to it again. All he needed was time.

Like an eternity.

He was still holding the soap, letting the water run over his body without making any effort to wash away the effects of the long day's exertions. He put the bar against his chest, rubbing it slowly in a circular motion until the pulsing spray began to produce suds. He willed himself to stop the endless cycle of regret that played over and over in his head.

The noise of the shower door moving against its metal track was unmistakable. As soon as he heard it, his gut tightened with that same anxiety he'd felt walking into the restaurant yesterday.

"I thought maybe you needed your back washed," Andrea said, her tone light. Almost teasing.

He didn't turn to face her. He couldn't. Maybe if he didn't respond, she'd go away.

He closed his eyes, fighting a sting he hadn't expected. Then he forced them open, concentrating fiercely on the pattern of the ceramic tile in front of him as he blinked away the unwanted moisture.

"Duncan?"

"Go away, Andrea."

His voice was harsher than he'd intended. Maybe that was for the best.

"Look at me and say that." In contrast, her tone was calm. Soft. Reasoned.

There wasn't a reasoned thought in his head right now. There were, however, plenty of emotions churning around up there.

Desire. Need. Love.

And fear. So strong it almost dominated the others. It would have if they hadn't been so damned powerful. And too long denied.

"Look at me," she said again.

She put her hand on the back of his shoulder. A jolt of desire seared through his veins, driving the blood to his groin in a roar of sensation. He fought the urge to respond, moving his shoulder instead, so that her fingers slipped off the slick, wet skin.

"Go away," he said again, each word distinct.

If she didn't, this was a battle he would lose. And he couldn't afford that.

He pulled his eyes away from the tiles to focus them on the ugly, reddened scars. The results of that explosion in Iraq. And then on the truncated forearm, which ended two or three inches above the wrist.

Since it had happened, he hadn't been able to even imagine touching a woman. Or allowing her to touch him. And knowing Andrea...

"You said too much last night," she said.

She was right, of course. He had known then that confessing how he'd felt about her had been a mistake. He had used his guilt about Paul's death as a shield so long he had almost convinced himself that was the reason he had never called her. Almost.

In the back of his mind, the truth of what he'd told her last night had always existed, hidden and unacknowledged. *This* was never how he'd imagined making love to her.

He took a breath, steeling himself for what he thought he would see in her eyes. He had no doubt it would be quickly controlled, but in that first unguarded second he would know.

He turned, no longer attempting to hide anything from her. Naked and exposed. Almost relieved to have this over and done.

He had intended to concentrate on her eyes so he could read what was in them. In the second it took to focus his gaze there, he saw too much. Enough to know that she was also nude, the smooth, olive-toned skin gleaming with moisture.

When his eyes found hers, there was nothing in them he could reproach her for. Nothing to feed his fear. Nothing but the same acceptance that had been in them when she'd laid her fingers over his.

And then they fell, slowly examining his body as if she were attempting to learn some new and difficult language. They touched on the scars, but they lingered over them no longer than on the hollow beneath his throat or on his breastbone or on the line of damply curling hair that led downward from it.

When her gaze reached the culmination of that, it caught and held. And as she raised her eyes again, they were filled not with the pity or revulsion he had dreaded, but with amusement.

"That doesn't *quite* fit with you telling me to go away."

He could deny with his mouth what he felt for her, but his body betrayed the truth. *Blatantly* betrayed it.

"I never said I didn't want you."

She nodded, lips pursing a little. "I don't think I've ever asked you for anything else."

There was a heartbeat of silence.

"Does that mean you don't *want* anything else?"

"No," she said, her eyes open and revealing. "I want whatever you'll give me. If that means I'm without pride, so be it. But...if I've learned nothing else, Duncan, I've learned that life's too short for cowardice."

The word wasn't accusatory, but it hurt. If there was one thing he had prided himself on through the years, it was courage. Enough to meet any challenge, no matter the danger or the cost.

"You think I'm *afraid?*" he asked, stung.

"Are you?"

The resulting silence was probably as revealing as her eyes had been. He should have found some facile lie to fill it. Although he'd been lying to himself for five years, he had never before intentionally lied to her.

"Last night, when you confessed you were terrified," she said, "I thought that was the bravest thing I had ever known anyone to do."

"I was terrified," he said, remembering, unwillingly, those first months of adjustment. "There are so many things—things we do every day, things we never even think about—that require two hands."

Unconsciously he lifted the shortened forearm, and her eyes followed the movement.

"Last night, in that hotel room, that was all I could

think about—'' He stopped the words, hearing the echo of that fear in his voice.

"I know," she said softly. "Actually...I don't *know*. I can imagine, but I guess that's not the same."

Her hands moved, their palms turning upward. The same gesture of resignation she had used when she'd talked about what had happened to her grandparents. *Life is too short for cowardice.*

The water, pulsing against his back, had grown cold. As the temperature inside the enclosure dropped, the steam began to dissipate, leaving behind it a vague sense of loss.

"I don't think making love requires the use of hands, Duncan. They would be helpful for some things, but...they aren't required."

It didn't sound like any kind of ultimatum, but he had known from the first that she would never beg. This would be her final offer. She had said that she would accept whatever he wanted to give her. And what he wanted to give—

He swallowed against the thickness in his throat. He knew what he wanted to give. And he knew what he wanted in return. All he had to do was find the courage to admit those two things.

"Look, Ma," he said softly. "No hands."

The shock he'd expected in her eyes when he'd turned to face her, revealing a body that could only be considered grotesque, was suddenly there. And then, being Andy, she did exactly what she was supposed to do. What he had intended her to do. She laughed.

"You think this is like riding a bike?" she asked. "Once you learn how—"

"God, I hope so," he said. "It's been…a long time."

She smiled, but there was a suspicious glint of moisture in her eyes, quickly controlled. "Me, too. You think we'll remember where everything goes?"

"I think it will probably come to us."

He reached out, cupping her face with his left hand. His thumb traced her cheekbone and then touched her lips, following the line of them. She smiled at him again, but she didn't move.

"It's cold," she whispered.

He reached behind him and shut off the water. The sudden silence after its noise was almost awkward. She shivered, hunching her shoulders against the chill like a child.

There was nothing else childlike about her. Again, consciously this time, he let his eyes study the slender curves of her body.

"Duncan?"

"Be sure, Andy," he demanded softly. "Making love to you isn't going to be enough. It isn't going to be all I want."

"Whatever you want to give," she repeated. "Whatever part of your life you're willing to share. I've loved you for a very long time. Even when I didn't know I did."

He took a step toward her, and she moved as well, so that their bodies were almost touching. If he had leaned forward another inch, her breasts, their small dark nipples hardened with the cold, would brush his chest. His erection tightened with the thought of their touch.

He tilted his head, aligning his mouth to fit over

hers. She looked up at him, her eyes wide, the fan of lashes that surrounded them darkened, spiked by the moisture.

He put his hand on the wall behind her and slowly lowered his head. Her lips parted in anticipation. She put her hands on his shoulders, stretching upward to meet him.

And everything he'd anticipated seemed to happen at once. The slide of her breasts against his chest. His erection touching her belly. His tongue moving to meld with hers.

Beyond thought or fear, he put both his arms beneath her hips, lifting. At the same time, he bent his knees, trying to deepen the contact between their bodies.

Her arms went around his neck as he moved between her thighs, pressing her against the sweating tile at the back of the stall. His chest, slick with soap, slid over the smooth, giving contours of her breasts.

"Yes," she breathed, her mouth against his cheek, her hand finding his erection. Holding it. Positioning it. "Yes, please."

With one hard thrust he was inside her. She gasped, breath warm as she hid the small, involuntary sound against the curve of his shoulder. Her legs fastened around his waist, and her mouth opened against his skin, teeth finding the ridge of his collarbone as he pushed deeper within her. And then deeper still. So deep that it seemed he had found the boundaries of her soul as well as her body.

On some level he was aware of the possibility that he might be hurting her. As the thought formed, she used the muscles in her thighs, wrapped tight around his waist, to slowly raise and then lower herself into the next motion.

The gasp this time was his. As was the moan that followed. Low, almost guttural. She moved in response, internal muscles caressing, drawing him inward. Inviting him.

His hips rocked upward. His hand found the softness of her breast. His thumb teased, flicking back and forth over the peaked nipple as his fingers cupped the outside fullness. Her breathing grew ragged, ratcheting inward in small inhalations beside his ear.

And then her body tightened around his again, the wave of sensation echoing along each nerve pathway nature had devised. Sliding over each engorged vein. Against each millimeter of sex-dampened skin.

"Andy," he groaned.

A warning he had no words to express. Only her name was in his head. And in his body was a roaring urgency to spill his seed into her welcoming, caressing warmth. To let go. To finally find the release that had been denied him through the long years he had known and wanted her.

He had *always* wanted her.

With that admission, whatever control he had spiraled away. His body convulsed, his hips driving again and again into the delicate softness of her body. And he was powerless to prevent what was happening.

As the rush of sensation began to explode, he had time to regret that he would leave her behind. Then, unexpectedly, he felt an answering paroxysm begin to shiver through her body. Giving him permission to stop fighting his own. Together their bodies strained in unison, individuality lost in a primitive and ageless duet, choreographed before time began.

It seemed to go on a long time. The surge of heated moisture fueling the endurance of his arousal. Her teeth and nails scoring the unprotected skin of his shoulders and back.

The spread fingers of his left hand griped, too tightly, one smoothly rounded cheek of her buttocks. His other arm tightened around her, seeking a deeper closeness. To become one. Joined.

Slowly, slowly, the shimmering ecstasy faded. Their bodies relaxed against one another. Her hands, which had only seconds before clawed at his back, soothed over its shivering muscles instead. His knees trembled with exhaustion, and he became aware, for the first time, of how tired he was.

After a moment, she lifted her head, putting her forehead against his. Their breathing still sawed in and out, almost in unison. Almost one.

Eventually, her legs released their hold around his hips. As she slid down the front of his body, an aftershock rippled through him.

He had believed he was incapable of further sensation. He had been wrong. And when she realized that, she lifted her head.

Her eyes seemed unfocused, drugged with passion. And more exhausted than they had appeared earlier, when he had been so concerned about her fragility.

There had been nothing fragile about the woman he had just made love to. Her responses had been as powerful as his. As deeply felt.

He had told her that she had been a good partner

today. That's what she had been tonight. A partner. An equal.

Her lips closed as she studied his eyes, and then slowly they began to tilt at the corners.

"What?" she asked.

He shook his head, too emotionally and physically drained to form words. They wouldn't be coherent. There was only one thought that echoed in his brain with any clarity.

"Marry me," he said, and had the satisfaction of seeing her eyes widen, the pupils expanding quickly into the rim of color. "Now," he added, his breathing still irregular.

Only breath enough for the essentials. And this was.

"I love you," he whispered, remembering that he hadn't told her that, and it was essential, too. Maybe more than the other.

"Yes," she said, answering the first before the second had registered.

It didn't matter. Nothing mattered but the lesson every experience in his life had conspired to teach him. One he had finally learned only today.

Life *is* too short—and far too precious—for cowardice.

Epilogue

The conference room at Blackheart, Inc. was tastefully decorated. Everything Ferris Blackheart did was tasteful, Patrick Blackheart thought, including the wedding she was in the midst of planning for her stepson and his fiancée.

Duncan Culhane and Andrea Sorrenson had already been ushered in, and he noticed the same subtle, love-flushed look in their eyes that he'd been barely tolerating in his son's inimical gaze. They were holding hands, an interesting fact, since Blackheart had already ascertained that Culhane's right hand was a prosthesis. He must trust the woman beside him very much indeed.

The Lalique music box lay on a small square of velvet in the middle of the table, waiting for them. Such a small, pretty thing to be worth such a fortune. Andrea released his hand and picked it up, opening the etched, carved lid in wonder. The music danced out into the conference room, light, delicate, from another time and another place.

"It's beautiful," Andrea said. "My grandmother will be so happy."

"Where did you find it?" Culhane asked. "When Griff called and said you wanted a meeting, I had no idea you'd managed to recover it."

"We recovered everything," Blackheart said calmly. "The rest of the Norenheld Treasure will be kept off the market while art historians do a thorough search of the original owners, the works will be auctioned off and the money given to the Holocaust Remembrance Museum."

Andrea Sorrenson was crying. "How can I ever thank you?" she said.

Blackheart didn't tend to appreciate tearful women, but he decided Andrea Sorrenson deserved a little slack, considering what she'd been through during the last few days. Considering what she'd accomplished without flinching. "It was the least I could do. I should have realized something was going on with Helms in the first place. I've survived by my instincts, and this time I ignored them."

"At least he's dead," Andrea said with a certain amount of grim satisfaction, and Culhane came up beside her, sliding his damaged arm around her waist with a natural gesture.

"Imagine that. What an amazing piece of luck, to have him shot by one of his own guards," Blackheart said lightly.

Culhane stared at him, a warning look on his face. "There must have been some kind of internal fighting."

"Presumably," murmured Blackheart, who knew exactly what had happened. "I guess there's only honor among thieves, not among terrorists. But he's dead, and the movement has been dealt a major blow.

Maybe not a mortal one, but it will take time for them to regroup. And plenty of people will be watching their every move.''

''I can't thank you enough, Mr. Blackheart,'' Andrea Sorrenson said. She was wearing a pearl and diamond ring on her left hand, a new acquisition since he'd first met her. It matched the glow in her eyes.

''You already did, Mrs. Sorrenson,'' he said.

''There's something you're not telling us,'' Culhane observed.

''If you have any other questions you can ask Griff Cabot,'' Blackheart said. ''But I really don't think you'll care one way or the other. Justice has been done, the bad guys are dead and everything's been taken care of.''

''Has it?'' Culhane said suspiciously.

''Indeed. Let me see you out,'' he said smoothly.

Andrea had already placed the fragile crystal box back in its velvet wrap, and she held it with both hands, almost as if she were afraid to let go of it. And then she looked at Culhane, clearly wanting to hold on to him as well.

Blackheart could see the thought flash through her mind as clear as day. She held out the fragile box to Culhane. ''Would you carry this for me?''

He looked at her in open astonishment. She'd already taken his good hand in hers, and he had no choice but to use his prosthesis. He was very good with it—no one but someone as observant as Patrick would have even realized there was any difference between his two hands. And then he reached out and took it, gently, carefully, and tucked it in his pocket.

Blackheart led them through the busy outer office

to the front door. The painter had just finished chiseling off the old name, and was in the midst of the elegant gold lettering of Blackheart and Son, Inc., and he was more than ready to see them on their way when Andrea Sorrenson took his hand in hers. "I wish there was something I could do to repay you," she said in a low voice.

"You already did," he said with a faint grin. "Nice shootin', Tex."